Branches

Rebecca Sloan

To Angela, who has made my life possible

ISBN: 1480297348

ISBN-13: 978-1480297340

...dreams have fragile walls
and often decompose into a silent dust
while reality assumes another form.

Contents

PROLOGUE

"I turned in my resignation this morning," I told Roland at the end of the spring semester.

"Why the hell you want to mess everything up? We got house payments and car payments. We can't afford to have you playing around with your...." He hesitated, searching for the right word.

I waited to see what he would come up with. I didn't expect it to be complimentary. The word he finally spit out was, 'hobby.'

That stung.

"It's not a hobby," I shouted defensively.

"Whatever it is, I don't want you to do it."

"It has nothing to do with you."

"It has everything to do with me. We got bills to pay. You can't afford to go crazy just because you want to do something *different*."

He had taken my heartfelt confession that I wanted to try something different before it was too late and made it sound ugly as the word snarled out of his twisted mouth.

"It's not crazy and you know it," I snarled back.

"Get real! How many little black Rembrandts do you think are running around in this world?"

Ganzie helped me sort it out. She listened patiently and then asked, talking to me like I was still a little girl, "What do *you* want to do, Sweetheart?"

"I don't know," I replied.

"Teaching is a wonderful profession. Lord knows, I gave enough of my life to it. But if it doesn't make you happy, don't be afraid to try something else."

I don't know if she was talking about my job or my marriage.

Now I walk into the Howard Ad Agency and I have no idea that the man who will become my boss will also become my lover. As unhappy as I am, I can't imagine making it worse. I think I've hit bottom and the only way is up but I don't actually know what bottom is yet.

1 Neely, 1975

A heavy summer rain pelts the ground, saturating the grass, turning soil into mud and streams down the sidewalks and streets into gutters in a wash of currents. Wave after wave of precipitation sweeps across the roof driven by large gusts of wind and the house vibrates in a steady rhythm. An explosion of thunder wakes me with a jolt. It's 7 a.m. in large, green, blaring digital numbers. The last time I looked at the clock, it was 6, so somewhere between 6 and 7, fatigue finally found me and pressed me into a deep sleep. Now my head is full of cobwebs and I don't know why the alarm is going off. My hand automatically reaches for the snooze button and slams it hard. Then I push my head deep into my pillow and try to shut out reality.

In a few minutes the alarm synchronizes with another angry blast from the sky and I realize it's going off because it's a work day. Reluctantly, I make a move to get up and a pain shoots through my side. Suddenly, all the events of the previous night come rushing back. I touch my cheek and it, too, still hurts from its clash with Roland's hand. Noises from the bathroom alert me that he's still in the house and I pull the comforter over my head, wanting to disappear beneath it, fearful that he will suddenly throw open the bedroom door and carry out his threat. My breathing comes in short, rapid intervals and I'm close to hyperventilation when the door between the house and garage slams shut. Only the humming of the motor of the garage door opener, the ignition of the car and the soft purr of his automobile backing out of the garage calms me down enough to think more clearly.

I need to get as far away from Roland as humanly possible. Even though I don't believe he'll really kill me, I need time to sort things out and decide what my future will be if I leave for good. The one person in the world who can help me figure out what to do is only a few hours away. I retrieve the suitcase from the basement and begin throwing clothes into it, not caring about wrinkles and creases, compelled by a surge of nervous energy. My destination is clear and I have to get there as fast as possible.

Ganzie.

She got that name when I was two and tried to put Grandma and Zelle in the same sentence and she's been Ganzie ever since. I've always run to her when things are bad and this time is no different. Whether it's a bruised knee or a bruised ego, she can make everything feel better. She's only scolded me once and I'm sure I deserved it but, in the end, I knew she understood and that's all that mattered. I had been disrespectful to Mama and she hit me with a fly swatter. Insulted and inconsolable, I took the money from my piggy bank, tucked my doll under my arm and prepared to hit the road. I don't know what would have happened if Ganzie hadn't intervened. She brought me to Sedalia, gave me a couple of weeks to settle down and then sent me back home but not without some straightening out of my attitude. She made it clear that what I had said ("you can't tell me what to do") was not a proper way for me to talk to my mother.

'She may not always say or do what you would have her say or do but she's your mama and you ought not sass her that way...or any grown-up for that matter. When you're a grown-up, you can do what you want but for now I expect you to behave yourself.'

Then just before I got on the bus, she took me into her arms and gave me a big kiss, saying, 'I'll always be here for you, baby, no matter what you do.'

Now my life is out of control again and I need Zelle Sims more than ever. To see her, to talk to her, to be protected by her, to know she loves me no matter what I've done.

I shower quickly, wanting to get on the road as soon as possible. The warm water feels good on my painful side and for a moment I allow myself to relax. But as soon as I'm dressed, the sense of urgency returns and I head for the garage, everything I want to take either in the clutches of my hands or slung over my shoulder, the car keys gripped between my teeth. As I pass the desk in the hallway, I think about leaving a note for Roland, but decide against it. I don't want him to know where I am. I throw my things into my car and back out of the driveway feeling like I am leaving the whole world behind me and yet leaving nothing at all.

The streets and sidewalks have been cleansed by the early morning downpour but the rain is softer now and the August air is cooler and fresher than the day before. Now that I'm on my way, I'm feeling better, like a heavy weight has been lifted from my shoulders. Going to Sedalia is the right thing to do and I'm anxious to get there.

I decide to stop by the office to tell Gill I'm leaving. We're right in the middle of a major ad campaign and he deserves a reasonable explanation, one that doesn't include my encounter with Roland. But when I get there, I can't face him, look him directly in the eye and hide the truth. Though my whole life feels like one big lie, at least between us there has been honesty and respect and I want to keep it that way.

Erica is at her post so I can't slip in and slip out without being seen. Forcing myself to sound as natural as possible, I speak too quickly.

"Erica, I'll be out of the office for a couple of days."

Erica, who never puts her nose in anybody's business, takes one look at my face and asks with great concern, "What's wrong, Neely?"

Covering the bruise on my cheek with my fingers, I avoid the big question mark in her eyes. "I just need to get away for a few days," is all I say.

"Where are you off to?" she persists.

"To see my grandmother."

"Is she ill?" Erica's hand rests just in front of the telephone console and I'm afraid she might pick up the handset and call Gill.

"No, I just have some things to talk over with her."

"What should I tell Gill?"

"Don't tell him anything," I snap. Then more softly, with a pleading look in my eyes, I add, "Please don't tell him anything. I'll call him later."

Once alone in my tiny office, I throw the drafts for the ad campaign into my briefcase and toss in some art supplies. Coming to the agency is perhaps the best thing I've ever done for myself...and the worst. My work life and my love life are hopelessly entangled in the person of one Gill Howard and I don't know where one ends and the other begins. I look around the room like it's a place I'll never see again. Perhaps I'll never see Gill again, either.

I leave just as quickly as I arrived, fighting back tears I don't want to shed, feeling badly about leaving without any explanation, knowing Gill will wonder why I didn't show up for work. And he'll be worried.

After work, he'll stop by Dinado's, hoping I'll be there to offer some sort of explanation. After he's fairly sure I'm not going to show up there, either, he'll stay for awhile longer, have a few drinks, throw a tip on the bar and then head for home. Once home, he'll fix another drink, turn on the TV and stretch out on the couch, falling asleep before the 10 o'clock news is over. Around midnight, he'll wake up and wonder what the hell is going on. He might even consider calling me but he won't because he won't want to cause me trouble. No, he definitely won't want to cause me trouble. And he'll have no idea of the trouble I'm already in.

It will be a strange night for a man who thinks everything is just fine with us and won't be able to figure out why I have vanished with no warning.

I'm sure of these things because Gill is a known quantity, a dependable accent to my life. But even knowing I could trust him and feeling the pain I'm going to cause him, I don't have the strength to explain my fight with Roland to him.

What little energy I have must be reserved for getting on the road while I still have the ability to drive. Anything else is just too much.

But one thing I'm not sure of: if I leave, will I have anything to come back to? At the moment it doesn't matter so I get in my car and head south.

2 Running Away

The drive from Des Moines to Sedalia is a familiar one. Highway 65 stretches out in front of me like a gray ribbon to the horizon. I can almost close my eyes and still keep the VW in its proper lane. The familiar route gives me time to think about all the mess I left behind. My cheek still feels the palm of Roland's hand and every time I move, my side reminds me of how hard I hit the floor. But the thing that sticks the most is his threat to kill me. As I think about what he said and how he said it, my foot presses harder on the accelerator to get me further away from him.

I drive fast and carelessly, the speedometer registering 85 miles per hour at one point, and I don't know how long I've been driving that fast. I slow down but soon am speeding again. Tears brim my eyelids and spill down my cheeks with little provocation and I don't really care how fast I'm going. Each mile brings another dreadful image: my parents, so cold and distant; crazy school days where I never belonged; then condescending Roland who tries to destroy me just because he can. Now the little good I had in my life has gone to crap and nothing will ever be good again.

I'm crying so hard I can't see the road so I pull into a gas station and just sit for awhile. Thinking. Which is the last thing I should do. Regretting. Which is also the last thing I should do but I've made such stupid choices or in some cases no choice at all and I regret it all. Always taking the short cuts, never considering the consequences, always latching onto whatever would make me feel good.

This time it backfired. What started out as pure pleasure is now causing extraordinary pain.

Why? Why? Why? There are no easy answers but Ganzie will help me figure it out, Ganzie will make everything right again.

I look up and see a phone booth. For a second, I think about calling Gill, but I stop myself. I'll talk to him soon but right now I'm not ready to explain my actions.

It rained off and on all morning, but the afternoon sun has dried off the pavement and drenched the day with heat instead of moisture. The coolness of the morning is gone but I'm glad it's hot, glad to feel the warmth soaking into my body, glad I can feel something other than pain. I feel better and decide it's time to get back on the road. I pull away from the telephone booth and continue south.

After the fight with Roland, I couldn't sleep and now it's caught up with me. I am so tired and I can barely keep my eyes open. It's a fight to stay in control of the car and of myself. But I have to get to Ganzie in one piece so I must stay alert.

At Chillicothe, I have covered more than half my journey and decide to stop again. I'm not crying any more but am still driving way too fast. If I don't slow down, I'm bound to get a ticket, or worse, end up in a ditch somewhere in the steaming expanse of northern Missouri.

I get gas, go to the restroom and dab my face with a paper towel drenched in cold water. I am almost too tired to go on but I can't stop, have to keep moving, have to get to Ganzie.

Maybe coffee will help and I buy a large cup and drink it black. Then I glance at my watch. It's 3:10 p.m. I hope to be in Sedalia before supper and it looks like I just might make it.

The house in Sedalia was built in 1910 by my grandfather, Charleston Sims, who died before I was born. The original floor plan included only five rooms: a living room, dining room, kitchen and two bedrooms. The structure is simple and functional, each room warmed by all the things Ganzie has acquired over a lifetime. The small bathroom, added some years later, still boasts the original fixtures.

"Even though we both worked, we were poor but Charles always made sure I had what I needed," Ganzie once told me. "He built this house with his own two hands so I would have a decent place to live. I thought it was too extravagant and I didn't want him to do it but he insisted and now I'm glad he did because it's all I have."

Now almost 90 years old, she seldom ventures out of the house that has sheltered her for all these years. Many times, Mama has tried to convince her to move to Des Moines, but Ganzie is so fiercely proud of not only her home but her independence that she wouldn't even consider it. And secretly I'm glad she has refused to leave Sedalia because it gives me a place to visit when I need to get away from my crazy world. I've been able to leave my frustrations behind, collapse into Ganzie's arms for a day or two and return home refreshed and ready to resume my life.

But I haven't been here for three years, just before I started seeing Gill, and I realize how neglectful I've been. I've shown little concern for the woman I profess to love so much and I have no idea if she is still capable of responding to my crises.

When I drive down the asphalt paved street and see the little house nestled behind a burst of shrubs, I feel the peace of being on familiar territory. I step onto the porch and the boards squeak in protest. I was so anxious to get here and now I hesitate. I should have let her know I was coming but I didn't so I can only hope my arrival won't be too much trouble.

I ring the doorbell.

3 Ganzie

Time has put the distinctive mark of aging on my body and the person who opens the door is a frail counterpart of the woman I was in my youth. My tall thin frame is now gaunt and stooped and my rich copper complexion is faded and sallow. My eyes, once exuding strength and courage, are weak and watery as I try to make out who is standing in front of me. When I realize it's Neely, I gasp in surprise then my whole face brightens into a smile. I am so happy to see her.

"Neely, baby," I say, almost in a sigh. "Where did you come from?"

"Oh, Ganzie, I've missed you so much." She grabs me and tries to pull me close but the sharpness of my shoulder blades causes her fingers to recoil. Not wanting to hurt me, she nevertheless holds on too tightly, and I wince at the pain.

"Is something wrong?" I ask, pulling back to look at her face. It's apparent she's been crying. And then I notice the bruise below her left eye.

"Don't you think it's time for a visit?" she says without looking me in the eye.

I take her hand and lead her into the living room. "How was the drive?"

"Not bad. Some rain then it cleared off."

"I don't have much food in the house," I say almost absentmindedly. "You should have let me know you were coming."

"Don't worry," she replies, glancing around the living room. I'm so glad Mrs. Dixon was here yesterday, straightening and cleaning for me. Not even a newspaper is out of place. "I don't need much," she adds.

"We can put your suitcase on the sleeping porch." I reach for her bag.

"Oh, no you don't," she rushes to stop me. "It's too heavy for you."

"Nonsense. You think your old Ganzie can't carry a few pounds?" I start to lift the blue and burgundy overnighter and it's immediately apparent that the weight is more than I can handle. I feel a twinge in my back that makes it difficult for me to straighten up.

Neely rushes to take the bag from my hands, laughing, "You know I never could pack light."

"Go check the linens in the extra bedroom. I think they're clean. And then we can talk about grocery shopping."

I find my way to the couch and sit gingerly so my back doesn't pull. I hate being old but even more I hate losing my health. The years went by so quickly and I never imagined that I would someday be not only old but old and decrepit.

I am thinking about Neely and why she's here—just out of the blue with no warning and with great big bruise on her face. Lord knows, she's more like my child than the child I raised and I've always wanted to protect her from all the hurts in the world. But she's a grown woman now and I may not be able to protect her anymore. Fortunately, she hasn't needed my help for such a long time. I miss it and yet I don't. It's hard to be responsible for someone else's happiness.

I hear her moving around in the bedroom and I think I should go to her. She may have things she wants to talk to me about but I also have things I need to say to her. Perhaps this is the time to tell her the truth about things. But it's such a hard truth and I don't know if I have the strength to form the words in my heart, let alone allow them to leave my lips. But I don't know how much longer I have and the secrets that are buried in my heart are begging to be free. I want Neely to know the truth and there's no one to tell her but me.

4 Neely

The back bedroom is really a sleeping porch with a wall of windows and a door that opens into the back yard. For as long as I can remember, I considered it my sanctuary. Now, as I walk through the dining room and down the short hall, I don't feel frantic anymore. Fortunately, the years have not changed it much. The three windows are still covered with sheer white curtains and the double day bed is still draped with one of Ganzie's handmade quilts. The scratches on the antique mirrored dresser are still concealed by a large hand-crocheted doily.

The room is filled with so much peace, I can almost reach out and touch it. I sit on the bed and don't move for a long time soaking in the warmth. Then I get up and go to one of the windows and draw the curtain aside. The lawn is unexpectedly neat, showing signs of a recent mowing and weeding. Many a morning, I escaped through the door to play on that cool green grass. Most times Lily Dixon from next door joined me and with our legs tucked beneath us, we sat on the damp carpet not even noticing the grass stains building on our legs. We showed off our dolls while searching for four leaf clovers among the blades of grass, tasting the pungent wisps of mustard seeds or biting into the sharp rods of rhubarb that grew on the edge of the back yard.

Ganzie also had an apple tree, a grape vine and a small strawberry patch. Lily and I picked and ate the fresh fruit without giving a second thought to dirt or germs. We didn't talk much about our separate lives. I kept my troubles to myself and Lily was quiet about the life she led when we were not together. Instead, we laughed, told stories of school and favorite subjects and far away dreams. It was a simple bond derived simply from the pleasure of being in each other's company.

Once Lily told me I was lucky to have a grandmother to travel to visit. Her grandmother lived with them and she had never known what it was like to take a bus trip to do anything, let alone visit a grandmother. Now she is off in New York being a successful writer and has probably traveled everywhere. We haven't shared a laugh for more than 20 years.

The summer I was ten I arrived in Sedalia with my arms wrapped around Jessie, my cheeks stuffed with anger and resentment vowing never to leave. The reason was simple: Mama had issued a command that I refused to obey. When she insisted on compliance, I replied, "you can't tell me what to do," standing my ground with great defiance. Then she slapped me, striking hard and quick in a fit of temper. Worse, she struck with the flat side of a plastic fly swatter, adding insult to injury.

The wound went deeper than the sting of the swatter and I made an instant decision to leave, calling Ganzie with tears stumbling my speech to describe my getaway plan. I would wait until morning, pack a lunch and then catch the 8 o'clock bus to Sedalia and I was never coming back.

"Let me talk to your mother," she said and I reluctantly handed the receiver to the angry woman at my side.

"I can't handle that child," Alma yelled into the phone so loud it made me jump. "She is headstrong and willful and has no respect for me."

"I'd say headstrong and willful runs in her blood."

"She told me I can't tell her what to do," Alma shouted, causing Ganzie to move the receiver away from her ear.

"Calm down, Alma. You've lost control of yourself."

"Mama, I will not let her talk to me that way."

"Look, I'm too far away to solve this. Put her on the bus. Some time and distance may help the situation. But let me tell you one thing, you have no business hitting that child with a fly swatter to make your point. You were raised better than that."

"Mama, you don't understand."

"I understand all I need to understand and if something like this ever happens again, Neely won't have to come running to me. I'll come up there and get her myself."

In my heart of hearts, I smirked, so pleased to hear Mama getting a scolding from her Mama. That was the way she talked to me and she deserved a dose of her own medicine.

Ganzie met me at the bus station and caught the steel scowl I had worn all the way from Iowa to Missouri. This wouldn't be an easy time, not like all the other times I came to

Sedalia to visit. Those times were carefree when I would bounce off the bus gleefully and spend a few days or weeks having Ganzie brighten my world. This time there was no glee, no bounce and the light was dim.

Later, on the sleeping porch, Ganzie tried to console me. Hugging me warmly, she tried to make it all better.

"What's wrong, my child," she asked between hugs.

"She hates me," I sobbed.

"Your Mama does not hate you. She's not always easy to understand, but I can tell you she doesn't hate you."

"She slapped me with a fly swatter!"

"And what did you do?"

"Nothing."

"Nothing?"

"Well..." I hated to admit my contribution to the fight. "I kinda sassed her."

"Shame on you. You must never show disrespect to your mother."

"I'm sorry," I said, then added mournfully, "Do I have to go back?"

"Yes, you have to go back, Sweetheart. But I'll tell you what—you can stay for a few days and we'll make a new dress for Jessie."

Ganzie held Jessie up to the light and gave her a once over. The beige fabric skin left over from a quilting project and the black yarn braids, remnants from an afghan crocheted years before I was born, were all showing signs of too many hugs and too many tears. The yarn hair was fraying, the hand-stitched seams were coming apart and the hand-painted eyes and mouth were fading.

"She looks pretty good for her age," Ganzie laughed. "But maybe she needs more than a new dress."

Over the next few days, she gave Jessie a new life as she mended the seams, re-painted facial features and re-braided hair. Out of a few scraps of nothing, she created a beautiful new dress complete with matching slippers.

"What do you think?" she chuckled.

I didn't smile but I felt better. Just having Ganzie be the one in charge of things had improved the situation.

"Things will feel better with some pie in your tummy, don't you think?"

Soon she had me eating her peach cobbler and laughing and my upside down world was righted once again.

I look out over the back yard and remember a lifetime of Ganzie setting everything right again but now perhaps the tables are turned. Maybe, this time, Ganzie needs me.

On the way back to the living room, I stop in the kitchen to check the refrigerator. It's nearly empty. Only a few slices of a loaf of bread, some margarine on a glass dish, some jam in a half-full jar, a few eggs and some orange juice in a carton. I'm not surprised because Ganzie is so thin, like she doesn't eat much at all. In the past the refrigerator would have been stuffed with leftover roast chicken and dressing, a half-eaten cherry pie, potato salad, bologna, cheese, dinner rolls and there would have been ice cream in the small freezer compartment. There would have been enough to eat for several days without ever leaving the house. Now as I look at the meager rations and consider Ganzie's frailness, I know something is terribly wrong.

Ganzie is waiting for me on the living room couch, her face uplifted and full of smiles. I sit next to her, take both her hands into mine and kiss her on the forehead. Then I say firmly, "I want to know how you've been, Ganzie, and I want the truth."

"You worry too much about nothing," she replies simply.

"But, Ganzie, you have no food in the refrigerator."

"If I keep too much food around, it just goes to waste."

"You have to eat to stay strong."

"I don't have a big appetite anymore."

"Well, you must eat. What do you want for supper?"

"Get whatever it is you want, honey. Don't try to figure out anything for me."

"Chicken? You used to love chicken."

"That sounds good," Ganzie says with no enthusiasm.

"Good. I'll pick up some chicken and tomorrow we can go to the market together and get things you'd like to have."

"That'd be fine, that'd be fine."

"Do you want Original or Extra Crispy?"

"You decide, you decide."

5 Ganzie

The more tired I get, the more I repeat myself and tonight I'm exhausted. Each day my energy dwindles and each day I struggle to hang on a little longer. In spite of all my trials and tribulations, life has been good to me and I hate to leave it. But the doctor said it won't be long now and I am preparing myself to die in peace. It's hard to go from the known to the unknown but my faith in God gives me comfort as I face the inevitable.

I look at my beloved granddaughter and know I should tell her about the tumor on my lung but I can't find the words. Neely will be so upset and frightened that we'll never get to the things she needs to talk about. And I know she needs to talk. There's no way her tear-swollen eyes landed on my front porch by accident. Over the years she's been closer to me than my own daughter and I can always tell when things are going well for her and when she's in trouble. For sure, this is a time of trouble. The bruise on her cheek tells me something bad has happened between her and Roland. I haven't seen her for three years and even her phone calls have been infrequent and brief. And suddenly she's here. I know something is terribly wrong. And I know she's come for my help.

No, I will keep my secret for as long as I can and give her time to tell me what's going on.

But tell her I must because I know so much about the harm that secrets cause. Most of my trials and tribulations were because of secrets, those of others, especially my Charles who for a time, lived a double life and managed to keep me totally in the dark. And then there were my own secrets, ones I kept from him and ones I buried in my life as if they would never resurrect and hurt anyone.

But secrets never die. They lie in the subterranean cavities of the soul and wait for the day you're at a low tide and then they pounce. In the meantime, they touch your life and every life you touch with their malignancy. But a secret revealed is a secret that no longer has the power to do any harm. That's why I must tell Neely the truth before it's too late.

6 Neely

Seeing Ganzie's eroded strength is almost more than I can bear. Reluctant to leave, I back my car out of the driveway and head in the direction of Kentucky Fried Chicken® hoping, if I can make Ganzie eat, her vitality will return and everything will be all right. But over plates of fried chicken, mashed potatoes and biscuits, Ganzie only picks at her food and I don't eat much myself. My heart bleeds for her and I feel a great distance from the woman I love. I try to bridge the gap with a distant memory.

"Do you remember that time I was mad at Mama and wanted to come live with you?"

"Indeed I do. You called and said you'd be on the next bus to Sedalia...and you were." Then she added, laughing, "You were such an intense child."

"I wanted to come live with you forever but you wouldn't let me stay."

"You're my favorite grandchild but I couldn't let you leave your mother that way."

"I'm your only grandchild so I'm certainly glad I'm your favorite," I tease.

Ganzie purses her lips as a thought crosses her mind, then flickers quickly away. "Indeed, indeed," is all she says.

"You should have let me stay."

"You were such an intense child," Ganzie repeats.

"After I got back home, I tried to make the best of it but it was never easy."

"That's what we all do, Neely. Make the best of things and keep going. Your mother was wrong but so were you. We all make mistakes."

"My life is one big mistake," I say bitterly. "It's falling apart and I don't know how to stop it."

"And you're worried about me?"

"Don't tease, this is serious."

"So when are you going to tell me what's so serious?"

I take a deep breath. "Roland and I..." I pause and Ganzie is watching me intently, waiting for me to continue. "...are having problems," I finally get it out.

"What kind of problems?"

"Big ones."

"Problems can be fixed, problems can always be fixed."

"Not these."

"They must be pretty heavy then."

My problems are, indeed, heavy but how am I going to tell Ganzie? The one person who can guide me to safety is too sick to come to my rescue. But Ganzie loves me no matter what I've done; she will help me if she can. I take another deep breath and let out the words slowly on the exhale.

"He hit me last night," I finally get out, moving my fingers to my cheek to cover the spot where Roland's fist connected with my face. Though the swelling is minimal, the sensation is as fresh as if it just happened.

"I hoped you got that bruise from bumping into a door," Ganzie says sadly.

"Please don't ask me what I did to deserve it," I say just as sadly.

Ganzie doesn't say anything and I struggle to continue. "And he threatened to kill me."

"Oh my..." she says as her jaw goes slack and her watery eyes widen with astonishment.

"I left because I was afraid of what would happen if I stayed."

"I had no idea things were so bad."

"They have been for a long time but this is the worst. This I don't know how to handle."

"I don't want you to think I'm not on your side, Neely, but it takes two to break up a marriage. Are you telling me everything?"

Just like when I was 10 years old, I am trying to solicit Ganzie's help by stacking the deck in my favor. But this was more than a slap with a flyswatter and I need to tell her everything. "I'm in love with another man," I say quickly, running the words together in my haste to get them off my tongue.

Ganzie raises her eyebrows and shoots a glance at me but says nothing.

"I'm in love with another man," I say louder and more pointedly.

"Yes, yes, I heard you. I may be old but I'm not deaf."

Neither of us says anything for a minute and then she asks pointedly, "So is this why Roland hit you?"

It was more of a statement than a question.

"He doesn't know."

"Don't fool yourself, Neely. He knows. He may not know who or when or where or even why, but he knows. You can't have someone else in your heart and keep it a secret. He may not be sure it's another man but he knows something has come between you and he's smart enough to guess that it might be a man."

"Absolutely everything has come between us. I don't love him anymore, if I ever did."

"What's this young man's name?" Ganzie asks softly.

"Gill."

"And how long has this been going on with this Gill?"

I'm too embarrassed to answer.

"Is this why I haven't seen you for such a long time?"

"I didn't know how to tell you."

"Neely, I'm an old woman. Don't know how long I'll be on this earth. Don't ever stay away because you're afraid to tell me something."

"I've always been able to talk to you but this was different."

"Different?"

"He's my boss."

"That makes it very complicated indeed."

"And I was ashamed..."

"Yes, shame is a mighty heavy burden to carry but you can't live your life that way."

"I don't know what to do."

"I don't know if I can help you with this one, Neely, but I do know that when you finally make a decision, it will be the right one for you."

By 9 o'clock, I can tell that Ganzie is too tired to visit any longer. "Why don't you go to bed?" I ask, reaching to help her out of her chair.

"I hate to leave when you just got here." But she doesn't resist and struggles to stand up.

"Don't worry. I'll watch a little TV and then I'll go to bed, too."

Ganzie not only allows me to walk her to her room but she lets me slip her nightgown over her head. When I was a child, Ganzie tucked me in so many nights and this role reversal is difficult to handle.

"We'll talk more tomorrow, Sweetheart," Ganzie says as she makes herself comfortable under a blanket even though the temperature in the house is very warm. "I promise."

"I love you, Ganzie," I say, kissing her gently on the forehead.

"I love you, too, Baby."

7 Blame or Responsibility

Ganzie's bedroom is at the front of the house next to the living room so I keep the TV volume low, almost too low to hear it. I hope the background noise will be enough to put me to sleep but it isn't. I can't quiet the video in my head that plays and replays my fight with Roland. I've committed to memory every word that was spoken and feel the sensation of his hand connecting with my face. Each time I move, I feel the pain in my side and I am filled with both fear and loathing. How am I ever going to straighten out the mess I'm in?

And Ganzie isn't well. How could I have brought this burden to her doorsteps? I should leave right now and drive back to Des Moines rather than worry her. But I can't leave, don't have the strength to face my problems by myself and I hope Ganzie will forgive me for being so selfish.

Exhausted, I stretch out on the sofa and sink down into the oblivion of the soft cushions. My eyelids are heavy and my head aches and still I can't let go and fall into a merciful sleep. For awhile I follow the story line of the late night movie but it isn't compelling enough to hold my attention. Memory, sadness, fear and anger all mix together and tighten around my head like a vise.

I try not to think about Gill but, of course, as soon as I let him in my head, he's all I can think about. I miss his soft voice and the feel of his hand on my shoulders when we're talking. I miss his smile and the touch of his lips. I really miss the way he makes me feel like I matter. That, in the office and in his life, I am important. But I never expected to love him the way I do and I have no certainty that he's worth ripping the seams of my life with Roland. I guess I should have thought of that before I started down this path because the life I've been so carefully protecting is over. It vanished so quickly I'm not sure it ever was. I should have divorced Roland a long time ago, now I have no choice. Everything I've worked so hard for is gone, gone, gone. I have only me to take care of me, only me to make me happy, only me to make all my decisions. I'm not sure how to do any of it.

When I wake up, the Today show is playing on the TV and I'm still on the couch. Somewhere between the late night movie and 7 a.m., I must have fallen into a deep sleep even though it feels like I didn't sleep at all. My dreams were full of Gill and Roland and the disaster of my life that it felt like obsession, not dreaming. I stretch, yawn and bring myself to life. There's no movement from Ganzie's room, so I get up, take a bath and throw on some fresh clothes.

In the pantry I find an old electric coffee pot that looks like it hasn't been used in years and a tin of ground coffee that's been languishing in the freezer. I finally find some filters stuffed into the back of a drawer so I scrub out the pot and brew some coffee. With a hot, steaming cup warming my hands, I go back to the living room and watch the rest of the Today Show waiting for Ganzie to wake up.

Patience has never been my virtue and the wait is interminable. The television again is not enough of a distraction to keep me from thinking and I quickly slip into a blue funk.

How did I let this happen? How could I be so stupid?

I can't blame Roland because he didn't live up to my idea of a perfect mate. Naïve and full of unrealistic expectations about romance, I walked into marriage with blinders on. Had my eyes been wide open, I would have seen that Roland now is very much like Roland then—vain, opinionated, arrogant and egocentric. But in the beginning, the end was not in sight and everything was obscured with optimism and not to be seen for what it was.

He was the Big Man on Campus and I was the shy pretty girl from the Midwest. There wasn't any reason for us to even talk to each other and yet we did. And when he asked me for a date, I considered myself the luckiest girl in the world. Sometimes I thought he was acting on a dare; other times I thought he really liked me. It didn't matter. I was so flattered by his attention that I didn't ask questions.

One date led to another and soon we were a steady couple. I fell in what I thought was love very early on and for reasons I still don't understand, he said he loved me, too. But love comes in many illusions: mine was feeling safe and wanted; his, I believe, was in having a pretty wife who would never challenge his authentic masculinity.

A year later when he proposed, I believed I had achieved my destiny.

"Marry me, Neely,' he said, kneeling in the classic pose. "You are the perfect woman for me." What he meant was, 'You'll look good on my arm and you won't be any threat to my ego.'

"Yes, of course," I replied, trying to calm my bursting heart. What I meant was, 'You'll take care of me and I'll never have to be afraid again.'

Those words highlighted everything that was wrong about 1959, a time when being dependent wasn't a bad thing for a woman to be.

And I can't blame my parents for my screwed-up life. They were as good to me as they knew how to be. Measured by a material yardstick, I had a great childhood. I lived in a nice house, wore nice clothing and usually got what I wanted even though I often had to do a lot of begging and crying to get it. There are people in the world who don't have enough to eat so I was lucky in spite of what seemed to be lacking.

So if I were to judge myself honestly, I'd have to call me spoiled. Spoiled and unrealistic and never having to face any real dangers or hardships. No wonder things are so tough now. I've never developed any survival skills. Tough enough to break my marriage vows but not even half tough enough to survive the consequences. Spoiled and unrealistic, that's what I am.

I get up and open the front door. The day is already showing signs of intense heat and I try to catch any breeze that might blow across the porch. My VW is parked in the gravel driveway and, for a minute, I consider leaving. My eyes follow the street all the way to its vanishing point and I imagine myself disappearing into its shadows.

At 8 o'clock I hear noises coming from Ganzie's room. Relieved to no longer be alone with my thoughts, I go to the bedroom door to find her up, dressed in her robe and making her bed. Her trembling fingers pull clumsily at the sheets and bedspread and she is almost too frail to complete the task. I quickly move to help but she raises her hand in protest, continuing to smooth the fabric as she puts her pillows in place, patting them deftly when the job is finished. Only then does she look up and smile at me.

"Good morning, sweetheart," she says with genuine pleasure. How did you sleep?"

"I fell asleep on the couch," I reply, giving her a kiss.

"You never did want to get up and get in the bed."

"Apparently I haven't changed much."

"I had a good rest last night," Ganzie offers. "It must be because you're here."

I smile, pleased to know my presence has made a difference. "I made some coffee. Would you like breakfast?"

"Just some toast to go with that coffee. I'm sorry there's not more here for you."

"Don't worry about me, I'll go to the store later. Do you need help getting dressed?"

"Thank you, no. I still do a pretty good job of caring for myself. My bones just move a little slower these days."

I help her to the kitchen, settle her into a chair and put a cup of steaming coffee on the table in front of her. I go over to the toaster and drop bread slices into the slots and catch

Ganzie in my peripheral vision as I wait for them to pop out. She is just sitting there, not moving, not sipping her coffee, not paying any attention to her surroundings. I go to her and take her frail fingers into my hands. My words are firm but gentle.

"Tell me the truth, Ganzie. You're not well, how are you managing to keep things going?"

She replies in a steady but weakened voice. "The Dixon's help out and they take very good care of me. They even make sure I get to church on Sunday when I'm up to going and they get me to my doctor's appointments. They're very good to me."

"Does Mama know?"

"No, and I don't want her to. I've taken care of myself all my life and I don't want her to interfere."

"She has to know! Maybe she needs to move you to Des Moines and have you seen by a doctor there." Tears flood my eyes and Ganzie pats my hand lovingly.

"That's exactly what I don't want. I've got more doctors here than I can shake a stick at. Besides, I don't want to leave my home.

"But Mama would love to have you in Des Moines. And so would I."

"And do what? Sell this house and be a burden on her? On you? That's precisely why I don't want her to know. And what would you do with me around all the time? You don't need an old grandmother to worry about. You have enough on your plate as it is."

"But the house, it's too much for you."

"It's all I have. I want to stay here until I can't anymore."

She doesn't say she wants to die in her own home, but I understand that's what she means. "And how long is that?" I ask.

"I don't know, Neely, but things are not as bad as they seem."

I am overwhelmed with the reality of losing Ganzie and I am visibly distressed. Ganzie struggles to get up from her seat and put her arms around me just like she did when I was 10 years old.

"Don't be so upset. We all get old. I'm lucky to have lived such a long, full life."

"How long has it been this bad?"

"It's been a gradual thing. Some days I feel like my old self and then some days I can hardly get out of bed. It's been worse lately."

"I'm so worried about you," I cry, bearing Ganzie's weight as she leans into me for support.

"And I'm worried about you," Ganzie says with a decisiveness that tells me the subject is closed.

8 Ganzie

By late morning Neely has gone to the market alone. I didn't want to go and she understood. I use the time to look for some old photos I want to show her because I'm more certain than ever that I'm going to tell her the truth. It's been festering in me for too many years and if I go to the grave bearing the weight of its secrets, my soul will never rest in peace. I'll be turning over in my grave for an eternity to pay for my sins.

I am resting in my room when she returns, her arms full of bulging grocery bags. I follow her to the kitchen and we chat while she puts the food away. Cookies, crackers and dried fruit go in the pantry. Apples, oranges, carrots, potatoes, and baked chicken go in the refrigerator. And an apple pie goes smack dab in the middle of the kitchen table. She seems so satisfied with her purchases and all I can think is who's going to eat all that food.

"I got enough for you to have after I go back," she says.

I know I look sad but I can't help it.

"You won't eat it, will you?"

"Won't is too strong a word, Neely. I just can't eat that much."

"If I fix something light, will you try?"

"Maybe some tea and cookies. That actually sounds tasty," I say, actually meaning it. I feel so much better since Neely's been here. Maybe part of my illness has been just plain loneliness but I'd never admit that to a soul. I've been alone all my life, even when I was with other people and most of the time I like it that way.

Neely makes me a cup of tea and puts a plate of sugar cookies on the table. "I haven't had tea and cookies for as long as I can remember," I say, picking up one in my small, bony fingers. "These look delicious. It puts me in mind of when Grandpa Charles was alive. He loved tea and cookies—any kind of cookie but he preferred oatmeal."

Then I add with a sigh, remembering Charleston Sims more favorably than usual. "I wish you could have known Grandpa Charles. He was a good man...and so handsome. I think you two would have gotten on well together."

By mid afternoon we're on the sofa and I'm wondering where to begin. I need to say just the right things to help her through her crisis and to prepare her for another crisis that she has no way to know is coming. I feel stronger than I have for a very long time. I hope it's enough to get through this.

"Now we can talk," I say matter-of-factly, covering her long, beautiful fingers with my gnarled, old hands.

"You don't have the energy to deal with my problems," Neely says sadly.

"I may not have much energy but I'm willing to listen and help the best I can. Trouble is, my help may not be enough."

"Just being here is helping."

"Are you planning to go back?" I ask calmly as if we had been talking about it all along. Once before, I made Neely go back and face her problems. And now, just as then, I half hope she'll stay.

"I have to go back. I have a job and a home. Well, I don't guess I have a home anymore, but I have a job. Yes, I have to go back, but I don't know what to do. I feel like I'm falling apart."

I look at her with great compassion and gently ask, "Do you love this Gill?"

"I think so."

"I'm talking about love, not passion and not romance."

"When I'm with him, it feels like love."

"Let me tell you what I believe love is," I say whimsically. "It's like a good, hot meal when you're hungry and got your mouth set on something special. It satisfies your soul and makes you strong enough to keep going. But passion and romance are more like chocolate cake and ice cream—they raise your blood pressure and make you fat."

Surprise catches Neely by the chin and she looks at me like I just slapped her in the face.

"You don't take this seriously, do you?"

"Of course, I do. I just think you shouldn't take it so seriously. You can't do your best thinking when you're backed into a corner. You're not the first person with this dilemma and you won't be the last."

"That doesn't help much, Ganzie," she says angrily.

"Of course, it does, if you look at it the right way. We all have things to figure out. Once was a time when women did what we were told but I think we should do what we think is best for us."

"But Roland hit me..."

"And you have to keep yourself safe first of all. After that, what you do is up to you."

"Please tell me what you think I should do."

"You're not a child, any more, Neely. I can't give you a hug and a kiss and make it better. So I'm talking to you woman to woman. That's what you need right now. Straight talk."

She looks very upset and I fear I have hurt more than helped. Truthfully, the things I want her to know will hurt even more but she has to know the truth and there's no way to protect her from any of it. I wrap my arms around her and pull her close.

"Don't cry," I whisper.

We stay that way for what seems like hours because my arms begin to ache. I give her a reassuring squeeze and kiss her forehead.

"Let me tell you something else you should know. A little chocolate cake and ice cream never hurt anybody."

Neely laughs like she's about to choke.

"Oh dear, I've said the wrong thing again."

"You just seem to be making fun of something that hurts so badly."

"Yes, I know it hurts. It always hurts when we want things that aren't good for us. Fortunately, we don't get everything we think we want." My voice trails off at the end of the sentence like a memory fading away into nothingness.

We fall into silence. I know Neely is hurting but I don't know what else to say. Sometimes I think it's a woman's lot in life to hurt. I still hurt after all these years and I don't know if my words are meant to give comfort to Neely or to myself.

When she finally speaks, her voice is weak. "All I've ever wanted was to be happy," she says.

I look at her thoughtfully. "There's nothing wrong with wanting happiness. Don't be so hard on yourself."

"Maybe if I stop seeing Gill, I can make things right with Roland."

"Maybe. Maybe not. Sometimes two people just aren't meant to be together."

"You mean me and Roland or me and Gill?"

I look at my lovely granddaughter and I'm not sure what to say. She wants answers and she thinks I have them. But if I did, I would never have married Charleston Sims. He and I weren't meant to be together but I tried to fool the gods and married him anyway. All I ended up doing was fooling myself.

9 Neely

Ganzie's life with Grandpa Charles was right out of a fairy tale: he literally rode into her life on a horse and whisked her away. I've seen photos of him perched atop his roan stallion and he was quite a handsome sight—tall with smooth light brown skin and a square jaw centered by a strong, proud chin. I'm sure she fell in love with him at first sight.

And he loved her. From the stories I've heard, he was devoted to her, risking life and limb to be with her and take good care of her. He even built this house with his own two hands to make sure she had a place to call home. And when he died, he left her enough money to see her through the rest of her days. Maybe they fought—who doesn't? Maybe they had hard times—who doesn't? But they raised a daughter and made a life together for over 30 years until the day he died. Theirs was a romance made in heaven. What can she possibly know about whether two people should be together or not? Charleston was the love of her life and she didn't have to live everyday regretting her decision to marry him.

The lateness of the afternoon darkens the room. The evening paper hits the front porch and nearby a dog barks. The unexpected sounds assault the silence in Ganzie's living room.

"Love is a good foundation," Ganzie continues, "but trust is more important. You can't love someone you can't trust."

"I don't know if I trust Gill."

"Every man will do something to cause you doubt. It's hard to find love, passion, romance and trust, all in the same man."

The same man.

The words hang in the air like a mist I can feel but not see.

The same man.

Was Gill that man? Maybe.

Had Roland ever been that man? Definitely not.

Fourteen years of marriage have stretched to the breaking point whatever was been good between us. How would those fourteen years have been if I had been married to Gill instead?

The same man.

I think about Grandpa Charles. Had he been that man for Ganzie? When I ask, "Did you find them all in Grandpa Charles?," I am really thinking out loud and am surprised to hear Ganzie's voice reply, "That was a long time ago."

I snap out of my reverie. "I'm sorry."

"No need to be sorry. It's just hard to remember that far back."

10 Ganzie

I close my eyes because I can't look at Neely. Alas, I remember it all and time has not diminished the intensity of my feelings. In the quiet hours of my lonely old age, I think about it all too often. My thoughts rake back over the years to the past and I am again a young girl with my whole life ahead of me instead of an old woman about to die.

I still see Charles riding his horse down the lane to my front porch. He usually came to call in the early evening after a long day's work. I was always waiting for him on the steps. Just about this time of day.

In the beginning, I loved Charles more than life itself. I would have done anything for him. But things change, sometimes so much that the beginning gets lost in everything that follows. And then history is lost and the bonds that tie us all together are based on lies. That's why I have to tell Neely the truth. She has a right to know her history and there is no one else to tell her.

If she had not come to me at just this time, I might have taken the secret to my grave. But here she is, just at the moment she needs to be. It's meant to be...and I alone have the power to give answers to questions that she hasn't asked.

The doorbell rings and breaks the mood. Neely goes to answer it and Mr. Dixon is waiting on the porch with two plates of food.

"Howdy, Neely," he greets her in his folksy way. "I thought when I saw that car with Ioway plates that you mus' be here. Mizz Dixon tole me to bring y'all some supper."

"That's very nice of you, Mr. Dixon," Neely says. "Ganzie and I have just been sitting here talking and time got away from us." She takes the offered plates.

"I hope it ain't too hot for you. August in Mizzouri can be steamin'."

"Iowa's not much better so I'm used to it. Would you like to come in? It's a little cooler in here."

"No, but thank you kindly just the same. We onliest wanted to make sure Mizz Sims is doin' ok." Then he peeks in the door past Neely and says, "Howdy, Mizz Sims. How you be tonight?"

"I'm fine, Mr. Dixon. Happy to have my granddaughter here."

"I know you are. How long you gonna be here, Neely?"

"Probably till Sunday—think I'll head back on Sunday." Then she asks, "How's Lily?"

"She is just fine," Mr. Dixon says with a wide smile.

"Where is she now?"

"She's way off in New York. Doin' real good. She sure will be tickled when I tell her I seen you."

"Tell her hello for me."

"That I'll do."

"Tell Mrs. Dixon hello," I say, not wanting to be rude but wanting to end the exchange. Neely and I have some serious talking to do and I need to get on with it before I lose my resolve.

"That I'll do," he says, then adds, "If y'all need anythin' a t'all, just let us know."

"We will. Thanks so much," Neely says.

"G'night, Neely. G,night, Mizz Sims."

Then we are alone again and Neely turns to me and asks, "Are you hungry, Ganzie. Mrs. Dixon fixed some tuna casserole and green beans. It looks real good."

"Oh dear, I'm still full of cookies and tea."

"Would you try a little?"

"If you insist," I acquiesce.

Neely takes the plates to the dining room and I follow slowly. Again we sit at my ancient table and I stick the fork into the tuna but don't take anything from the plate to my mouth. I really don't want Neely to know how little I can eat but I also know the time to fool her is long past.

"Try to eat the green beans at least," she chides me. "The Vitamin K will be good for you."

"Look who's the grown-up now," I say, laughing and sticking my fork into a green bean.

Our earlier exchange weighs heavily on my mind. I have so much more to say and so little energy to say it. She told Mr. Dixon she's leaving on Sunday which means I don't have much time. But it's so pleasant to be with her that I feel it's a good omen. Maybe time will stall for just a bit, long enough to give me a chance to enjoy her company before I spoil everything.

"Tomorrow is Wednesday already. Your visit is going so fast," I say mournfully.

"I don't know if I can leave you here alone."

"I'm used to being alone, Neely, and most of the time, I don't mind it at all." Suddenly I realize it's too late to start the story tonight. It's too long and I'm too tired. Tomorrow will be a better day to begin. "Do you mind if I go to bed, honey?" I ask.

The lightness in her voice does not match the worry in her eyes. "Of course not. I've got some work to do, anyway."

"Tomorrow, we'll talk some more." There. One more day before it all comes crashing down.

"I love you so much, Ganzie."

"And I love you, Neely."

11 Neely

For the second night, I put Ganzie to bed and am left alone with my thoughts chasing around in my head. Everything I have taken for granted is up for grabs. All my past decisions are fatally flawed and I fear there is no time to make them right.

Pulling the art supplies from my briefcase, I dabble at the ad project I was working on before I left Des Moines. Drawing is the one thing that gives me pleasure no matter what else is going on and, for a few hours, I am fully engaged in sketching ideas to promote borrowing money.

I make a list of the various aspects of the bank's business model: secure savings, easy mortgage loans, solid investments, excellent customer service, and I represent each in a simple line sketch, my signature style. I produce about 10 drawings that meet my satisfaction...and will please Gill as well...and decide it's enough.

Ah, Gill. My world of problems returns full force. I should call him; he'll be wondering where I am and if I'm okay. But what would I say? If I tell him about my fight with Roland, he'll go off the deep end. If I don't tell him, all my other words will get stuck in my throat.

Sleep is my only ally and for the second night, the couch is my haven. I want to be as close to Ganzie's room as possible, afraid that settling between the cool sheets on the day bed will lull me into a state of well-being that is non-existent.

Ganzie has not said she is dying, but in my heart, I already know.

The next morning I wake rested and hopeful. Something made sleep possible even though nothing has changed. For no reason at all, I feel free and easy and, for the first time in ages, I look forward to the day.

Ganzie is also in good spirits when she wakes up and I prepare a light breakfast of scrambled eggs and toast for us. "That was really good, honey," she says when she has eaten all she can and is sipping on a cup of coffee heavily laced with cream and sugar.

"You should eat like this every day," I tell her.

"If I ate like this every day, I'd be as big as this house."

"You don't eat nearly enough and you know it," I protest.

"Having you here has increased my appetite."

"I'm glad my visit is good for something."

She looks at me thoughtfully. "Come," she says, "let's take our coffee and go sit on the couch. I have some photos to show you."

"Photos? Of who?"

"Of me and your Grandpa Charles when we were younger than you are now."

She walks slowly to the living room and I follow, carrying a cup of coffee in each hand. A few feet from the couch, her steps falter and I quickly put the cups on the coffee table to come to her assistance. I hold her frail sides with my palms and gingerly lower her to the couch. I can feel her bones through the fabric of her dress and I shudder at how far things have deteriorated.

"Are you all right, Ganzie?" I ask, afraid to hear the answer.

"I'm fine, just felt a little woozy but I'm just fine now."

She takes both my hands into her own and holds them tightly. I can feel the coolness of her fingers and the lack of strength in her grip.

"I'm glad you're here, Neely," she says.

"I'm glad I'm here, too. I should have come months ago."

"Don't dwell on what cannot be changed. Don't ever do that! It'll zap the spirit right out of you."

I settle on the couch next to Ganzie and say softly, "I try not to, I really do. But sometimes I just can't let things go."

"I didn't say it was easy. I just said, don't do it." Ganzie then smiles at me in her whimsical fashion, an imp flashing just behind her eyes. The smile gives me more hope than I have any right to believe in.

"There are some photo albums on the chair in my room," she says. "Would you go get them for me?"

I retrieve two worn leather cases and set them on the coffee table in front of her. I have looked at the photographs before but now as she flips through the pages, they take on new meaning. There is an interesting anecdote about each one and Ganzie tells the stories as though I am hearing them for the first time. We are transported back in time and I willingly follow where she leads me.

Ganzie points to the one of Grandpa Charles sitting tall on a roan stallion that I have seen so many times before. He's wearing a Stetson hat and riding boots with overalls hidden by a dark double-breasted jacket. Ganzie stands beside the horse, her head at his knee, wearing a long-sleeved white dress, high in the collar, pinched at the waist and flowing to the ground. The photo is worn around the edges and parts of the picture are beginning to fade with age.

Ganzie continues, "We were engaged to be married when this was taken. It was the Spring of 1907. Charles was twenty-four and I was only twenty."

"You look beautiful," I say with awe.

"When your grandpa was around, I felt beautiful. But I was so young," Ganzie says, her voice in a trance. "So young and so ignorant, but of course I didn't know it then. I had been away to college so I thought I was all grown up."

I've heard the story about Ganzie's college days but like hearing it again. It makes me think of her young and vibrant, not old and dying.

"I went to Philander Smith in Arkansas and it was hard on Papa to have me so far from home."

"He didn't like to see his little girl grow up."

"Actually, he was more worried for my safety but I convinced him I would be as safe at a Methodist School as I would be under his watchful eye."

"And were you?"

"Times were tough for black folks everywhere, but no real harm came to me. I went with my friend, Birdie Smith, and we looked out for each other. Just a few insults now and then; nothing I didn't hear in Sedalia."

"Tell me the story about how you met Grandpa Charles," I say eagerly, wanting again to hear the romantic tale of how she was wooed by the handsome man in the photo. I wait for a response but Ganzie seems preoccupied with another thought. A long moment of silence passes and then I feel something else coming, something different than before, that this time Ganzie has another story to tell.

Ganzie hesitates, then begins to reminisce. "Papa, as you know," she continues, "was the local Methodist preacher and we lived just on the outskirts of town at the end of a dirt road called Maple Lane. The church was called the Maple Lane African Methodist Episcopalian Church and it was Papa's last assignment.

"Our house was on the adjacent lot which was a good thing because we spent a lot of time at church—all day on Sunday, Wednesday evening and any other time Papa thought we should be there."

She lets out a little laugh, remembering something from years ago, and continues.

"I met your grandpa at the Juneteenth picnic in 1906. Every year Black folks got together to celebrate the Emancipation Proclamation and that year it was hosted by our church.

"He was far and away the handsomest man in the area. And such a hard worker! Yes sir, handsome and hard working--a rare combination. I was considered fortunate that he picked me to court."

Ganzie removes the photo from the page and runs her fingers over the face of Charleston Sims. "I think I fell in love with his eyes. You can't see it in this photo but he looked at you in a way that made you feel like you were the only person in the world who mattered."

Her voice fades to a wisp, weakened by the power of memory. Then in clear, steady tones, she paints a portrait of a time long ago, a splash of colors she has carried in her heart for almost seventy years.

"Sedalia was a good town for black folks in those days with lots of railroad jobs and lots of colored businesses. Your Grandpa, he had a good job." Ganzie turns the page of the photo album and there is another picture of Charleston Sims standing in front of a half-built house.

"He was a carpenter by trade, one of the finest in the world. It wasn't an easy trade for a black man but there was a lot of work in those days 'cause they were practically rebuilding the whole town.

"That's this house in the photo. He built it himself, you know." Ganzie has a tone in her voice I've never heard before, somewhere in the space between reverence and remembrance.

12 Juneteenth, 1906

Sedalia, MO

Charleston Sims first noticed Zelle Marshall at the Juneteenth celebration in 1906 on a glorious day just meant for a picnic. Cascades of alabaster clouds raced across a cornflower blue sky partially obscuring a white sun keeping a warm day from plunging into stifling hotness. Crowds of Negro town folks and farmers assembled on the grounds of the Maple Lane AME Church to observe the day word of the Emancipation Proclamation first reached slaves in East Texas, an anniversary that was honored in Negro communities all across the country.

On long tables covered with red checkered table cloths, there was an abundance of wonderful soul food on display: fried chicken, glazed hams, barbecue ribs, potato salad, candied yams, corn on the cob, collard greens, macaroni and cheese, deviled eggs, fresh tomatoes, and for dessert, peach cobbler, sweet potato and minced meat pies and watermelon, along with pitchers of lemonade, iced tea and strawberry soda. Folks were laughing and singing and children were playing games. It was a day to celebrate despite the struggles Negroes everywhere still endured. It was a day to feel good about just being alive.

Zelle had just come home from two years in Little Rock and was celebrating her safe return to family and friends. She was only 19 years old but her face conveyed a certain regal confidence that made her appear wise beyond her years. Representing the A.M.E. church proudly, she greeted the guests and helped serve pastries at the dessert table.

It was not the first time Charles had seen her but it was the first time her beauty caught his attention and took his breath away. Tall and slender she was with a rich, copper complexion, smooth like hot chocolate with marshmallows. Her long black hair was caught at the nape of her neck with a red satin ribbon that matched the red ribbons running through eyelets on the bodice of her powder-blue dress.

Hypnotized by her beauty, he took his glass of iced tea and walked directly to the table where she was serving a generous portion of peach cobbler to a young man who seemed equally entranced by her charm. He waited until his potential competitor left, then indicated he'd like some cobbler for himself.

'Haven't seen you around these parts,' he initiated the conversation boldly.

'I've been away at college.'

'College?'

'Yes, I just got a teaching certificate from Philander Smith.'

'Went to Lincoln myself. Didn't finish, though. Like carpentry better.'

'You're a carpenter?'

'Try to be.'

'I admire a man who can build things,' Zelle said demurely.

Charles puffed up like a peacock and pronounced, 'Name's Charles Sims of the Sims Family Farm east of town. You probably heard of us.'

Zelle nodded her head. Yes, she knew of the Sims brothers. They had made a success of the small farm left to them by their parents, their mother dying when Charles was born and their father dying of a heart attack a few years later. William, the oldest, was then left to raise his siblings and work the farm. Their story was somewhat of a legend in the community but they went to the Baptist church and she had never seen Charles before.

'My name is Zelle Marshall,' she said dipping the spoon into the cobbler.

'You must be the preacher's daughter,' he said matter-of-factly, looking at her with an expression in his eyes that she would always remember even in hard times. In truth, he knew exactly who she was, having seen her with her Papa on several occasions. But that was a long time ago and the young woman smiling at him now was far more beautiful and alluring.

'Yes, I am,' she answered, looking at him warmly because Zelle Marshall knew no strangers, being equally kind and thoughtful to everyone she met. But this tall, handsome man gave her heart an unexpected leap and made the skin of her neck feel flush all the way to her cheeks.

'Nice day for a picnic,' he offered inanely.

'One of the best,' she said, her response casual but her eyes sparkling and leaving an indelible mark on his heart. 'Would you like some cobbler?' she added.

'It looks delicious.'

'My mama made this one,' Zelle pointed to the large pan of peach cobbler she'd just dipped her spoon into, the crust brimming with cinnamon-laced peach sauce.

'Then that's the one I want,' Charles said.

Zelle scooped a large portion of cobbler on a plate and handed it to Charles. He accepted it all the while staring into her eyes, trying to send her a message that he was interested in more than peach cobbler. But the young Zelle was too taken with the handsome stranger to notice that he was actually flirting with her.

'Nice meetin' you, Mizz Marshall.'

'Nice meeting you, too, Mr. Sims.'

Charles moved away from the table but for the rest of the afternoon, no matter where he was, Zelle was in his peripheral vision. He made a promise to himself that someday she would be his wife.

On the very next Sunday Charles, a practicing Baptist, showed up at the Maple Lane AME Church dressed in his best seersucker suit, white shirt, bow tie and straw hat. Only his dusty riding boots detracted from his gentlemanly appearance and indicated he had come a long way to attend the service. He sat inconspicuously in the last row and watched the proceedings but his attention was on the young woman playing the organ. Clad in a long black skirt and a puff-sleeved white blouse, Zelle wore her hair pinned up in a severe bun. It made her look older than her nineteen years, but she was nonetheless as beautiful as the week before.

Toward the end of the service, Rev. Marshall made the guest announcement. 'There is a visitor in the house this morning,' he said in a booming voice, 'and I ask, at this time, that you please stand up and give us your name and tell us your church home.'

An unembarrassed Charles stood up and stated clearly, 'Charleston Sims, Pilgrim Baptist Church, thankin' you folks kindly for your hospitality.'

Zelle looked over the heads of the church members to where Charles stood and her stomach fluttered with the awareness that he had come because of her. But on the outside she remained calm and composed, playing then for the choir the most beautiful notes, each one sent to Charles' ears as a clear indication of her pleasure at his being there.

'Maple Lane welcomes you, Mr. Sims. Come back any time you have a mind to visit us.' Then he bowed his head in prayer. 'Heavenly Father, we thank you for our guest, Charleston Sims, who no doubt traveled a long distance to be here today. We thank you for the safety of his arrival and pray for the safety of his return.'

The entire congregation replied with a resounding 'Amen' and the service ended with everyone rushing to Charles, shaking his hand and asking if he intended to join church. He tried to be polite all the while his eyes searching the crowd to see where Zelle was. Breaking away from the inquisitive parishioners, he dashed to the front door, thinking he had missed her entirely. Standing in a moment of despair, clutching his Stetson in his hand, he was prepared to leave when Zelle emerged from the church holding an arm full of sheet music. As soon as he saw her, he stepped into her view and asked, 'Can I walk you home, Mizz Zelle?'

Thinking he left without a word, she was delighted to see his tall frame standing in her shadow. Her laugh came with sparkling, crystal tones and she said, 'I just live over there,' pointing to the white frame house across the churchyard.

'Well, can I escort you to your front door?'

'Papa might not like it,' she said, disappointed because she knew it was so.

'I 'spect you're right. Just the same, it's mighty nice seein' you again.' He tipped his hat, stood patiently as Zelle skipped across the grass to her Papa's house, then got on his horse and rode away, whistling, smiling and feeling an extraordinary pleasure in his heart.

Rev. Marshall stood just inside the church watching the scene, not pleased to see his daughter being picked for courting, but relieved the man doing the picking was someone like Charleston Sims, a church-going young fellow with a reputation for hard work and thrift.

His wife, Sarah, a patient woman who had shared all his hard times and buffered all the wrongs he endured, moved to his side. 'It'll be all right, Clozer,' she said softly, patting his arm to calm him down. 'Really it will. It's time for her to find someone decent, just like I found you.'

13 Ganzie

The memory of Charleston Sims causes me both pleasure and pain. Over the years, I've tried very hard to focus on the pleasure but as I bring it all to the surface to tell Neely the truth, I feel the pain all over again.

"Your Grandpa came to church almost every Sunday after that. I was tickled to death but I tried very hard not to let it show."

"Did your Papa approve?" Neely asks with unbridled curiosity.

I don't respond to her question directly. Instead, I pick up another photo.

"This photo was taken on my 20th birthday."

"You look beautiful," she says. And it's true. At 20, I was probably at my best. And the photo gave me a look of sophistication that seemed more glamorous than I was. The photographer had posed me sitting stiffly in a fanned back chair and encouraged me not to smile.

"I wasn't nearly as serious as I look, but the photographer convinced me it would make a better picture if I didn't smile. Don't know why folks put so much stock in being stern.

Anyway, I had only seen your Grandpa at church a few times when I decided to ask Papa if I could invite him to Sunday supper. But Papa said 'no,' it wasn't proper.

"The next Sunday, I told your Grandpa what Papa said and he gave me an odd look, then said, 'I guess it's high time for me to make it proper,' and marched right back into the church. I followed because I couldn't imagine what on earth he was going to do.

"Papa was in the little room off the vestibule where he kept all his books. He was sitting at the small table where he wrote his sermons. His glasses were perched on his nose and his Bible open when Charles walked in and confronted him. Papa looked at Charles sternly and asked what he wanted. But I think he knew full well what it was about."

'Rev. Marshall,' Charles started bravely, 'I have come to ask your permission to call on Zelle. I have nothin' but the finest intentions towards her and I want to get to know her better. As you know, I'm a hard worker and a God-fearin', church-goin' man and I have the highest regard for you and your family. I would respect Zelle at all times.'

"Papa was flabbergasted. I was the oldest so he didn't have any experience dealing with such matters, but he could tell Charleston Sims was not to be put off easily."

'I s'pose this has somethin' to do with comin' to supper next Sunday,' Rev. Marshall said forthrightly.

'No, Sir, it's just high time you knew my intentions since I been settin' up in your church every week.'

'Well, Mr. Sims, you may as well know you're talkin' about my pride and joy when you're talkin' about my Zelle. Me and Missus Sims have done our best to raise a good Christian daughter. Sent her to a good school so she could be somethin' someday. We're mighty proud of her...'

'Yes, sir, I know,' Charles interjected.

'Don't interrupt me, son. I know my daughter full well enough to know she's taken with you and I could part the Red Sea sooner than I could steer her in another direction. You seem to truly be a hard-workin', church-goin', God-fearin' man, so I will tell Zelle she can invite you to supper but let me tell you one thing: if you ever so much as harm a hair on her head, you'll have more than God to fear.'

The conversation between Charles and my father rolls out of my memory with ease and, after all these years, I can still repeat it almost verbatim.

"Papa was such a gentle man," I continue, "but I think he put the fear of the Almighty in your Grandpa's heart that day. It gave Charles great reverence for Papa and later, when trouble developed, Papa was the first person he confided in.

"All through the rest of that summer Charles called on me. Whenever he could manage, he left his construction site early, rode five miles home to clean up and then rode the distance back to town. Supper was on the table by the time he came trotting down the lane on his roan stallion. He joined us for the meal, chatted with me for awhile and then was well on his way long before the late afternoon sun turned orange in the sunset.

"It wasn't safe for a black man to be on the road alone after dark and he gauged his time very carefully, making a great sacrifice just to be with me for an hour or so.

"Most of the time, however, we weren't alone. My younger sister, Ivy, often shared the porch—and the conversation—with us; and my baby brother, Jeremiah, planted himself on Charles' lap and demanded his undivided attention. To make matters worse, Papa himself came out on the porch, letting the screen door bang loudly behind him, if he thought anything at all was amiss.

"Only Mama took pity on us and eventually shooed the youngsters away or called Papa back into the house. Papa grumbled and reluctantly left us alone for a few minutes, then found his way back to the porch to light up his pipe.

"Occasionally we walked over to the big maple tree in the churchyard, but once there we were still in full view of the front porch so there was little chance for any hand holding and none for stealing a kiss. Only when he was ready to mount his horse and head for home did Charles dare lean over to give me a peck on the cheek."

14 Zelle and Charles, 1906

Charles, a quiet, self-contained sort of man, found it easy to talk to Zelle Marshall and looked forward to their conversations, however brief.

'I hear you come from a big family, Mr. Sims,' Zelle said to him early in their acquaintance using the formal address in such a way that was still quite personal. It was an effort to keep him at a distance, not allowing herself to think of him as a suitor. Later, it became a habit and through all their years together, she called him *Mr. Sims* in public and also in private when she was very angry.

'My mother died when I was born and my father when I was ten. William Jr. is the oldest and has worked real hard to keep us all together. We owe everything to him.'

'Who is we?'

'Me, my other brothers and my sister, Margaret.'

'Just a house full of ruffians, I'll bet,' she continued, laughing in a way that he found charming.

'A house of brothers with only one sister can be pretty rough, I guess, but we get along okay. We try to be civilized. Margaret may say elsewise.'

'And you're a hard worker, they say.' She smiled at him to let him know it was a friendly statement to get to know him better, not a personal query to measure his accomplishments.

'Work hard as the next man, I guess. Got no college education, but I can build anything that needs to be built.'

'A college education isn't everything,' Zelle said, even though for all her life her father had taught her just the opposite. But she didn't want Charles to feel that her education put her out of his reach.

'All my brothers were pushin' me to do somethin' better than farmin' so they sent me to Lincoln but I couldn't make it work. I studied hard for two years but it wasn't my cup of tea. I like to work with my hands, like the feel and smell of wood and I finally got into carpentry.'

'That's not easy work for a colored man.'

'I do okay. Got a pretty good business with a couple of fellows. Once in awhile, we get work with white crews. We don't always get treated well so we try to get our own contracts when we can. I make a good livin',' he added, to let her know he was substantial and could maybe support a wife.

Zelle blushed and changed the subject because marriage to Charleston Sims was not an idea she entertained in any serious way. She may have written 'Zelle Sims' in her notebook a few times but that was just for play, nothing she believed could ever happen.

'When I went to Arkansas,' she said, picking up the thread of one of his thoughts, 'I was not prepared for what life would be like away from home. We always stayed close to the school because it was unsafe to venture elsewhere. It was hard to be treated badly after living here and being so protected by Papa and his reputation.'

'I've never known that kind of protection,' Charleston confessed. 'I grew up knowin' what I could and couldn't do, when to speak and when not to speak, where I could go and where I dare not. William wanted to make sure none of us got lynched and he taught us to be strong but not act too strong in public.'

'That must be hard.'

'You learn. Trouble is, sometimes no matter how hard you try to stay out of trouble, trouble finds you.'

'Has trouble ever found you?'

'Not really. I've seen it, though. Seen plenty. More than I could tell a lady about.'

'I don't know much about life, Mr. Sims, but I know what it's like to be colored. Papa hasn't been able to protect me from everything. I've always known my place in this town and I know how to act in public, too. Sometimes it hurts, sometimes it makes me angry and sometimes I just don't care about things anymore.'

'Now, that's hard. How do you do it?'

'I don't know. I don't try not to care; it just happens.'

'Don't ever let the white man take your spirit from you, Zelle. It can happen but try to protect yourself from it. My sister went to St. Louis to get away from all that kind of mess.'

'I don't think you ever get away from that kind of mess, Charles. Colored is colored when all is said and done and little else matters.'

'If you were my wife, I'd try to give you all the things you want and I'd try to make you happy. And I'd protect you.'

Zelle heard Charles' words but certainly didn't take them seriously. It was a nice thing for him to say but she was not sure Charles could protect her because he probably couldn't protect himself if someone really wanted to hurt him.

Sundays were the best because time was more generous. Charles came to church services and stayed in town the rest of the day, having dinner with the Marshalls and spending an entire afternoon with Zelle. He was not a big talker and he didn't seem to mind that she was. Sometimes they played dominoes or checkers; sometimes he asked her to play the piano. He said he liked the way music filled the air just because she touched certain keys.

Other times they went back to church for special services. Whatever they did, they were drawn together in a way that all who observed them knew that something serious was happening. Zelle hoped that Charles was falling in love with her but she was more reserved about her feelings. She was determined to behave in a manner that her Papa would approve and she also wanted to protect herself from any hurt that loving such a handsome man could cause.

Dear God, she prayed each night before she drifted off to sleep, don't let anything take Charles from me. I think I'd die without him.

15 Winter Solstice, 1906

In the fall of 1906, Zelle began her teaching duties. Every morning she walked the six blocks to the elementary school where she spent her days teaching 4th graders out of books that had been discarded by the white school administration. Funding was poor for the white children; it was even worse for the colored. To control her seething anger at a system she could neither control nor influence, she tried to give her students more than what was offered in the books—a sense of pride in who they were and hope for a better future life. She was strict yet compassionate and her students fell in love with her.

Daily lessons were interspersed with real life stories of Negro achievements, stories she had heard from Papa and Mama and stories she had read about at Philander Smith.

'Booker T. Washington,' she told the class, 'is the greatest Negro alive. There are many who don't think of him in that light, but if you study his life, you can't help seeing the great contributions he has made to the colored people.'

Her opinions of Booker T. were formed from conversations with her Papa but after reading articles about him as well as those written by him, she, too, believed education was the means to freedom. His detractors called him an Uncle Tom but his most important message was to folks who needed to be uplifted. There were some who may not have needed his encouragement so much, but many were not that lucky. All she had to do was look around her squalid classroom to see how much support and reassurance was still needed.

'Caleb,' she called on one of her students,' "name one great thing Booker T. Washington has done.'

Caleb stood with pride to be the one singled out and said, with a beaming smile, 'He founded Tuskegee Institute.'

'Correct, Caleb, and that's probably his greatest contribution for if a colored man cannot improve his mind, he cannot improve his material condition.'

She looked around the small class of students and hoped that each of them could find their way out of poverty and degradation to a better world. They were all her children—Caleb, Elizabeth, Joshua, Bessie, Stella, John David, Morgan, Lester and the rest. She couldn't have loved them more if they were her own flesh and blood.

'You must always do your very best in your schoolwork so that one day, students in a school like this—well, not like this, because they will have new books and new writing tablets—but students just like you will be talking about *your* accomplishments and *your* achievements.'

"Each evening I went home, drained by the workday and frustrated by all the things I couldn't do for my students but I always looked forward to the next day when things might be better. Some nights I quilted; some nights I relaxed by crocheting or knitting, anything my fingers could do with my eyes almost closed.

"In those quiet times, I always remembered fondly the special things my students said or did...and then my mind inevitably drifted to thoughts of Charleston Sims. If I hadn't seen him for a few days, I missed him terribly. If I had just seen him that afternoon, I still missed him terribly. Many a doily grew into a tablecloth as my fingers continued the pattern past the finishing round while my mind soared in my love for the young man on the roan stallion.

"That fall, Sedalia had a building boom as many of the old brick structures were replaced with wooden ones. Most of the work went to white contractors, but there was always more than enough for Charles to do. In the push to get the outdoor work done before winter set in, his days got long and often it was near dark before he finished. With no time to visit, I felt like we were drifting apart. I tried to keep my feelings to myself but he knew how upset I was.

"In October a solution was offered that seemed at first to be a blessing but proved to be the beginning of a long, hard road for Charles to travel. Years later, when he tried to explain to me the decisions he made during those fateful days, he was hard pressed to determine what factors had influenced him the most."

16 Hollis McAdoo

Hollis McAdoo was Charles' best friend. They had known each other since they were youngsters and it was Hollis who helped him get into the carpentry business. Hollis wanted to start his own company and Charles was just the type of partner he was looking for--smart enough to do the paperwork and able enough with his hands to build a solid structure.

They had a successful business going but there were times they had to hire themselves out to white crews to make ends meet. Hollis hated it but Charles knew they had no choice. His brothers didn't mind the grit of rich black dirt under their fingernails but farming wasn't for him.

In October 1906, the days were getting shorter and night fell earlier and earlier. Charles and Hollis worked hard against time and disrespect to make enough money to see them through the long winter ahead. But staying cool in the face of daily insults was tougher than all the grueling work they performed. They often got the more dangerous jobs like roof shingling but they didn't mind because it put them at a height where they could see the whole city all the way to the horizon but more important, it removed them from direct contact with men who hated them.

'You know, they only letten us do this cuz we could fall off and break our necks,' Hollis smirked, swinging his hammer with the ferocity of a man seeking revenge.

'Yeah, but I like it up here,' Charles replied. 'At least we don't have to talk to them bastards.'

'You got that right.' Hollis swung the hammer and missed the nail head, hitting the wood instead. 'But I wish we didn't have to do this.'

Charles was more realistic. '*This* helps pay the bills.'

Hollis' anger was not to be abated. 'Bills or no bills, I don't like it. I'd like to get somethin' goin' like ole Atlas Ferguson.'

Charles had heard rumors that Atlas was moving up in the world but didn't know for sure what his good fortune was. He half hoped it was something he might be able to latch onto for himself so he could make marriage plans.

'What's he up to?' he asked with genuine curiosity.

'Got hisself a job runnin' errands for ole man Crawford.'

'Ole man Crawford, the banker?'

'Even gets to drive his new automobile...takin' him back and forth to the bank and such.'

That started Charles dreaming of a future better than the one he had been anticipating for himself. 'I'd like to drive an automobile someday but my own, not somebody elses.'

It was Hollis' turn to be more realistic. 'Maybe so...,' he started but didn't finish the thought. Then he added gleefully, 'But Atlas sure do like to drive that car. He say it makes the girls swoon.'

Charles laughed, 'I 'spect it does.'

'You know what Atlas call that car?'

'What?'

'He call it a Whippet cause he say he's gotta whip it to keep it going. He say the girls can walk faster than that car will go but they slow down just to be close to him.'

'Well, I'd like to have a turn drivin' a Whippet but I don't need no attention from girls. I'm thinkin' about gettin' married.'

Hollis stopped the hammer in mid air. 'Married? No shit?'

Just then, the Foreman appeared on the ground below and yelled up in a voice that was more of a warning than a question.

'Boys, what you all doin' up there?'

'Just finishin' up, Sir,' Charles yelled back while Hollis sent a fierce look in the direction of the voice.

'Well, get it done and get it done right. Got no time for yakkin'.'

'Yes, Sir, we'll get it done,' Charles yelled again.

Hollis whispered, 'Charles, I don' know if I can do this.'

'You can do this. Just keep quiet and let's get it done so we can get outta here.'

Then Hollis changed the subject. 'You headin' home tonight?'

'Yeah, but I'm hopin' to see Zelle for a minute.'

'Don' be too late on that County Road,' Hollis warned. 'They's a bunch of varmits out there that mean no good.'

'I haven't had any trouble.'

'You ain't had no trouble yet. Just be careful.'

It was only two weeks later that Hollis' warning proved to be something to take seriously. The day was Friday and the time was between late afternoon and early evening when the waning daylight made it possible to see the road clearly but it was also possible for danger to be lurking in the shadows.

Charles had stayed too long with Zelle and now it was near dusk as he made the trek home to the family farm. Knowing he shouldn't take such chances, his ears perked up at strange noises and his eyes were alert for any signs of trouble.

He pulled his coat together to stave off the nip of the late September air and urged his horse along the County Road galloping at a steady clip. Glad he had survived a tough week in one piece, his mind was on Zelle and the way her perfume made his ears tingle. He had only traveled a few miles further when two men on horseback loomed in the distance ahead. He dipped his head low and kicked the side of his horse to speed it up. One of the men yelled jeeringly to Charles as he passed by.

'Where you going, Boy?'

Charles knew better than to respond to such taunts and he maintained his horse's steady gait hoping that they were only out for a night of fun. But he couldn't be sure.

'Boy, we asked where you going,' the other man yelled, this time more insistently.

Charles was now well past the strangers and at first they made no attempt to chase him down. But just when he thought he was home free, he heard the clip-clop of horse hooves behind him. The men were closing the distance between them, continuing to call out to him and mock him. Their tone was derisive and their intention clear.

'If'n you come this way again, you best have a damn good reason. Else you best find yourself a diff'ernt route...'

Surrounded by the shadows of a looming darkness, a frightened Charles kept going, not stopping even for a breath until the family farm was in sight. Then, cheek muscles taut and eyes dilated with fear, he slowed and turned his stallion toward the oncoming threat. He made an instant calculation to face the danger rather than run from it. What kind of man was he if he was cowed by white trash? He had nothing to defend himself with but his bare hands and his lariat which he now gripped in anticipation of a defense maneuver. If they didn't outright shoot him, he believed he could prevail.

The men had also slowed and seemed to be priming for the onslaught. Then suddenly, one of them shouted, 'Shit, man, leave this niggra be. He ain't worth it,' and they turned and moved in the opposite direction, slowly as if they had just made a benevolent decision and had all the time in the world.

Gasping for air, Charles turned back toward home wondering what had scared the men away. Then he saw a flickering light and the image of his brother, William, coming down the road on horseback, carrying a lantern in his left hand, bracing a shotgun in the other. William waved to him with his kerchief, his arms making a broad swath through the air, signaling his baby brother home to safety.

On Monday he reported the encounter to Hollis. They were toting scraps of lumber away from the construction site, loading them onto a wagon and trying to stay out of view as much as possible.

'Had a close call last night, Hollis,' he said, keeping his voice low.

Hollis jerked his neck and looked at Charles with a knowing eye. 'I told you to be careful,' he said. Then he added, 'Anythin' bad happen?'

'Nah, they just tried to scare me,' Charles lied, not wanting to admit how close the call was. 'But I kept movin' and they didn't bother me.'

'You can't keep this up, Charles. You can't work late, see Zelle and still get home before dark. You might not be so lucky next time.'

'I gotta work and I gotta see Zelle.'

'Why don't you move to town for the cold season?'

Staying in town was the farthest thing from Charles' mind. But the chance to see Zelle every day was very tempting. 'Where would I stay?' he asked.

'There's a boardin' house over on Clark St. They's usually got some rooms.'

So it was Hollis McAdoo who suggested Charles stay in town for the winter. It was Hollis McAdoo who helped Charles find a room. It was also Hollis McAdoo who tempted Charles to venture into the nightlife of Sedalia and with whom he spent many hours in the Maple Leaf Club listening to Ragtime jazz.

And it was Hollis McAdoo who introduced Charles to his cousin, Ophelia Lucas.

17 Ragtime and Beer

The Maple Leaf Club was the hot spot in Sedalia. It was the place to be and anybody who was anybody stopped in to have a few drinks and spend the evening listening to lively Ragtime music. It was said Scott Joplin wrote the Maple Leaf Rag to immortalize the establishment though some said the club came after the success of Joplin's tune. No one knew for sure, but one thing was certain: the second floor club was a popular hideaway for anyone who had a liking for the sporting life. And so it was to the Maple Leaf Club that Hollis McAdoo enticed Charleston Sims on one of his first nights in town during the latter weeks of October, 1906.

The local ministers had tried to close the Maple Leaf Club and given his own devices, Charles would never have ventured into such an establishment. However, sitting alone in his small room on long, lonely nights evenings after spending too brief moments with Zelle, frustrated by a day of racial slurs and other indignities, tired of disrespect and belittlement, angry because he couldn't make an adequate living with his own company, Hollis persuaded him to go out 'to have a few beers and relax.'

'Com'on, Charles,' Hollis cajoled. 'Some of the best folks in Sedalia go to the Maple Leaf Club. There ain't no shame in havin' a few beers and listen' to a little music. Scott Joplin hisself wrote the Maple Leaf Rag 'cause he liked this place so much.'

'I've never been to a nightclub, Hollis, and I don't think I should start goin' now. Zelle would be through with me. And her Papa would kill me."

'No need for her to know, Charles. No need for her to know a t'all. You're just havin' an evenin' out with some friends. Ain't no shame in that.'

In the end, for reasons he didn't understand, Charles acquiesced and, to his misfortune, what he experienced at the Maple Leaf Club got inside his being and moved him in a way that nothing had ever done before. Church music had its way with the soul and took folks to new heights of emotion but this new music, this Ragtime rhythm and tempo that sometimes excited and sometimes calmed seeped into his spirit, mellowed his temperament and sent the cares of the day into the ether.

At first he ordered a beer reluctantly because it was what everyone else did but as the alcohol surged through his blood, he ordered another and then another, forgetting all about what Zelle and her Papa would or wouldn't like. He was enjoying himself so much that he wondered why he'd never done it before and couldn't wait to do it again.

Until the day he met Zelle, women had never interested Charles much. Sometimes he noticed a pretty girl but he never followed up on it. But on that day, he was hit by a thunderbolt and everything changed. He saw his life going in a certain direction and couldn't imagine it going that way without Zelle at his side. She was young, beautiful, accomplished, sweet, charming and innocent.

Everything a man could want in a wife.

Therefore, he was totally unprepared when Hollis introduced him to Ophelia Lucas.

'Oh, look, there's cousin Phelia comin' this way,' Hollis said. Charles, excited with music and warm with beer, looked up and saw a vision of beauty and elegance walking toward them. If a thunderbolt hit him when he first saw Zelle, he was now hit by the whole storm.

Ophelia was a stunning woman by any standards. Petite and lively and wonderfully clad in a green velvet dress touched with lace at the neck and wrists with skin the color of toasted walnuts. She floated toward the table of Charles and Hollis like she was moving on a cushion or air. Hollis asked her to sit down.

'Howdy, Phelia, what you doin'?'

'Not much, Hollis,' Ophelia replied in a silky voice with perfect diction. 'How are you tonight?'

'Doin' okay.' Turning to Charles, he said, 'Charles, this is my cousin Phelia. Phelia, this here is Charleston Sims, my business partner.' Then he added, 'Can you sit a spell?'

'My friends are just over there,' she replied. 'I don't think they would like it if I stayed away too long.'

Charles could smell her perfume and was taken with her soft voice with its proper accent. Unlike Hollis, who was almost illiterate, Ophelia spoke English impeccably and had a laugh that mixed with the music to create a whirlwind of sensations.

'They ain't gonna mind if'n you sit with your cousin for a bit.'

Ophelia sat down, visited with Hollis for a few minutes and then turned her attention to Charles. 'Why have I not met you before, Charles?' Ophelia asked in her satin voice.

Adrift on a strange sea, Charles tried to sound casual, not like he was in danger of drowning, but his voice belied his inner disturbance. 'I been around for a long time,' he said, brazened by alcohol. 'You must not be from around these parts.'

Hollis tried to interject, 'She just moved here from Texas,' but neither paid him any mind.

'I just moved here from Texas,' she spoke directly to Charles, ignoring Hollis entirely. 'I haven't seen you at the Club before.'

'I've only been here a few times,' Charles said reluctantly, not wanting to appear a greenhorn.

'Are you having a nice time?'

'I find it relaxin',' he replied. 'What brings you so far north,' he then asked, not wanting to talk about himself.

'My father came up to work on the railroad,' she said softly. 'I decided to come, too, because it is a hard life in Texas for colored folks.'

'It's a hard life for colored folks here, too.'

'It's a hard life for colored folks everywhere, but some places are better than others.'

'No place is better,' Charles said bitterly.

'My, oh my, you sound angry. If you're so angry, why do you stay?'

'I was born here, it's my home. Never been too far in any direction to speak of.'

'Well, this town is better than most I've been to. I know my place and I don't bother folks much.'

I'd leave if I could, Charles thought, but I wouldn't know where to go. Everything important to me is within a five-mile radius. How could I ever escape?

He studied the beautiful woman sitting next to him as if the answer was somewhere in her and she, in turn gazed into his eyes. When she spoke, she said simply, 'I must say, you are the most handsome man I've seen in Sedalia but I suppose you hear that all the time.'

Charles flushed as her compliment mixed with the liquids boiling his blood sent him reeling.

Hollis noticed the exchange with some amusement and decided it was time for him to leave. 'I'm gonna go have a dance. Do either of you mind?'

Getting no response from his cousin or his business partner, he muttered, 'Course, you don',' and he moved away from the table, glancing back only once to see Charles clearly entangled in Ophelia's web.

With Hollis gone, Ophelia renewed her assault. 'Don't blush, no need to be embarrassed,' she consoled.

Charles, not wanting to show discomfort, said staunchly, 'Yes, Ma'am, I mean no, Ma'am, I'm not embarrassed.' But he was and worse, he was drawn into the vivacious nature of Ophelia Lucas.

'Good, because I wouldn't want to ever do anything to embarrass you.' Then she rose up from the table, her fluid body rippling in her velvet gown and said, 'I must get back to my friends. It was nice meeting you. I hope to see you again sometime.'

Charles' nose followed the diminishing trail of her perfume as she walked across the room and his eyes were riveted to the graceful path she took away from him.

With Hollis' encouragement, Charles went back to the Maple Leaf Club again and again. He successfully split his life into two worlds: the one he shared with Zelle and her family and the new one of Ragtime jazz and beer...and Ophelia Lucas. If he had known how to detect trouble when he saw it, he would have stayed away from the Maple Leaf Club and the likes of such temptation. But he didn't know and Ophelia eased into his life quietly without any visible signs of intrusion.

18 Ophelia Lucas

It was a blustery November evening when Ophelia maneuvered Charles into escorting her home from the Maple Leaf Club. She had joined Charles and Hollis at their table soon after they arrived and then began chattering on and on about nothing in particular. Charles, as usual, listened attentively while Hollis, feeling like the odd man out, disappeared into the crowd.

Charles continued to sip his beer and let Ophelia flit from topic to topic without much response from him other than nods and smiles. He liked it that she did most of the talking and she liked the way he always showed an interest in what she had to say no matter how trivial. Only when she started talking about the new motorized taxicabs in town did Charles' interest perk up, always fascinated by talk of automobiles.

'We're getting to be like a big city,' Ophelia said.

'It won't change Sedalia that much."

'Of course, it will. It makes us modern and progressive."

'Will black folks be able to ride in them?'

'I think so; as long as they got a dollar in hand.'

Charles thought about the scarcity of the dollars folded in the bottom of his pocket and how rare it would be for him to take a taxi ride. As a matter of fact, he shouldn't now be spending his hard earned money on beer. He needed it for more important things, like food and rent and the church offering on Sunday. And to add to the stash he was trying to save for his future with Zelle Marshall. He was beginning to feel uncomfortable when he noticed Ophelia yawning.

'My, oh my, it's getting late,' she sighed.

Charles pulled out his pocket watch and flipped open the cover. It was, indeed, getting late and he knew he needed to get home.

'I wonder where Hollis is off to.' she said, looking around the room. 'He promised to take me home in one of those new fangled taxis so I could see what all the fuss was about but I guess he forgot.'

Charles wanted to come to the rescue but he knew he shouldn't spend any more money. Still he couldn't resist the opportunity to spend some more time with the lovely Ophelia.

'I guess I could take you home if you want,' he stammered, feeling unsubstantial in her eyes.

'I wouldn't want to trouble you.'

'It's no trouble,' he replied, feeling uncertain and as they stepped into the night air, the uncertainty grew into fear. Here he was, a simple man, with a beautiful woman at his side. Not to mention a simple man who was courting Zelle Marshall. He knew he should be anywhere but where he was.

At that moment a shot of cold night air swirled about them and Charles reacted immediately. 'It's chilly out here,' he said, pulling his coat off and putting it around Ophelia's shoulders.

Ophelia turned to him and smiled. 'Do you have enough money for a taxi?' she asked coyly.

He pushed his hand deep into his pocket, felt the skimpy wad of bills there and said, 'Course, I do.' Then he motioned to the driver leaning against an automobile. 'Can you give us a lift?' he asked the bulky Negro with a chauffeur's cap shading his eyes.

'Where to?'

Charles turned to Ophelia who said, '283 Broadway.'

Sitting in the taxi beside a beautiful woman he barely knew was awkward for Charles and words failed him. Ophelia boldly took his hand in hers to let him know she understood and accepted his silence. But making conversation was not his only problem. For the first time since meeting Ophelia, he had a strong sense he was doing something very wrong. Not quite sure of what to expect, however, he was unable to avert the peril that lay ahead.

When the taxi stopped in front of a small storefront shop on Broadway, Charles saw a sign above the door that said *Ophelia's Dresses*. He understood for the first time her expensive-looking clothing and her freedom to come and go as she pleased.

'So this is what the fuss is all about,' Ophelia said boldly. 'I could get used to riding in taxicabs.' She turned to Charles who was fumbling to take a dollar from his pocket and give it to the driver. 'Did you like it?'

Charles didn't answer, instead getting out of the cab and helping Ophelia step onto the curb, gathering up her long skirt in his hands to keep the fabric from dragging on the ground. The feel of the soft material caressing his fingers made him uncomfortable but he didn't know why. He motioned for the driver to move on and then he was alone with Ophelia with nothing to talk about.

'Guess I'll be going,' he said.

'You're going to walk?'

'It's not that far. I'm glad you enjoyed the ride. It was nice,' he said, finally answering her question.

'Won't you come in for a nightcap?' she asked innocently.

'I really need to get home,' he replied, quite sure that's exactly what he should do.

'Just for a minute? I won't bite.'

Hesitating, Charles nevertheless followed Ophelia as she opened the front door and stepped inside. Then she walked across a large shop area filled with fabric and sewing equipment to a back stairway. She turned and motioned Charles to follow.

'Well, Charles, here we are, this is where I live,' she said when they reached the upstairs residence, holding her arms up to indicate the expanse of the tiny living room. 'It's not much, but it's comfortable.'

'It's very nice,' Charles said, tugging at his tie and feeling strangely not himself, like he had been taken over by some alien spirit and he was no longer in control.

The room was, in fact, quite plain, but clean and neat. A striped Victorian sofa was the focal point, a wooden rocker sat unceremoniously in one corner and a large flowered rug covered the floor. The lighting was provided by a series of small wall lamps, each covered with petal shaped glass shades bathing the room in soft shadows that danced on the walls and on the drapes covering the large windows.

'I spend most of my time downstairs so it's not fancy. But this is home now and I like it.'

Ophelia was still talking and Charles thought he heard words like 'electricity' and 'plumbing' but truthfully he was no longer listening to what she was saying. Her perfume was so powerful and her skin looked so soft.

They stood in the middle of the room not moving to sit down nor toward each other. Those few minutes stretched into an eternity and Ophelia bridged the distance between them first. She moved closer to Charles and said softly, 'I don't have any beer. Would you like some bourbon?'

Momentarily coming to his senses, Charles said, 'I really gotta be goin'.'

'Don't go yet. Let me put on some music.' Ophelia moved away from Charles and suddenly the space between them was filled with a rush of air, as cold as the night outside. He watched as she put a disk on a Victrola atop a small table in the corner. Scratchy musical notes filled the room. She went back to Charles.

'Do you like music, Charles?' she asked.

'You know I do,' he replied.

'Let's dance,' Ophelia said, putting his arms around her small body.

Charles finally understood where the evening was headed and a jolt of electricity coursed through his body. He pulled away from her embrace.

'I should tell you that I'm seein' a young woman and I'm very serious about her.'

'We're just dancing, Charles.'

Ophelia leaned into Charles and kissed him on the mouth, tentatively but her intentions were clear. He almost fell over backwards in astonishment.

'I surely didn't mean to do that,' Ophelia lied, then kissed him again more assertively.

Very much against his better judgment, Charles' instincts carried him downstream with Ophelia as his guide. He kissed her back and then they were kissing each other with an intimacy Charles had never experienced. He was carried away by her touch and her perfume intoxicated him. Even Zelle's fragrance, which he thought was the most sensuous in the world, was no match for the power of Ophelia's scent.

'We can't do this, Ophelia,' he whispered, trying to pull away again.

She responded by pulling him toward her bedroom where she stripped herself of her fancy frock and helped Charles remove his clothing. Then she pushed him onto her bed and he found himself making love for the first time in his life. Most of the time he knew exactly what to do but when he faltered, she came to his rescue.

Ophelia consumed his senses, but flashes of Zelle interspersed with the powerful emotions that sent him thrusting into another woman's body.

And then all the feelings he had stored for Zelle exploded inside of Ophelia Lucas.

Later, alone in his room, full of guilt, he vowed never to see Ophelia again. Zelle would never forgive him but he vowed she would never, ever know.

Throughout the night, he wrestled with shame and humiliation. Toward dawn he realized he could not undo what had been done and there was only one way to make everything right: he must marry Zelle as soon as possible and begin their life together, the life he truly believed he wanted more than anything else on earth.

19 Ganzie

"We had kind of a rough winter that year," Ganzie says as she closes the photograph album and sits with her hand resting protectively on its cover. "More snow and cold than usual and not enough heat in the school to keep the children warm. We all huddled by a wood-burning stove while I tried to teach their lessons. Sometimes I think it made them work harder but I don't know for sure if that was true. I do know it made us close, just like a family. I wish I could have seen the future. I would have been more grateful for what I had."

I am puzzled by Ganzie's words but she makes no offer to explain. Instead, she continues as if nothing can stop her.

"Your Grandpa stayed in town that winter and it was so much easier to spend time together. He became just like family and everybody loved him, especially Papa. Most nights he came for dinner and he was at church every Sunday. Everyone assumed we'd be setting a wedding date; that is everyone but me.

"Papa was like the father Charles barely knew and they spent so much time talking politics and lamenting over the hardships of the colored man that I started having doubts that he really cared about me at all. So the night he asked me to marry him, it was a big surprise and very, very special."

Charles had planned to marry Zelle from the very first moment he saw her at the Juneteenth picnic but now was pushed by desperation to ask for her hand. He wasn't sure he was ready to give her the kind of life she deserved but he loved her and wanted her to be his bride. More important, he believed that if he buried the past, the future was still his.

It was an ordinary night and Charles was looking forward to dinner with the Marshalls and a chance to propose to Zelle. He had worked hard that day, gone home, cleaned up and rehearsed his speech. Zelle, as usual, was pleased to see him walking down the lane and ran to meet him, her eyes bright with joy, but totally unaware of his intentions.

'Let me help you with the dishes,' Charles said impatiently when he realized it was the only way he would be able to spend some time alone with Zelle. The whole family had unwittingly conspired to occupy the evening and soon it would be time to go home. He wanted to ask her before he lost his nerve.

'Have you ever washed a dish?' she teased.

He held up both hands and laughed. 'I've got two dishwashers right here.'

In the kitchen Zelle set up two pans of water on the kitchen table, one filled with sudsy water and one with clear water. She washed the dirty dishes in the sudsy water and then placed them in the clear water. It was Charles' job to rinse them properly, dry them and stack them on the counter.

But he took more delight in flicking Zelle with the flour sack towel than in applying it to the side of a wet plate. She had seen him in playful moods before but that night it irritated her. She took the towel from his hands and started drying the dishes herself.

Making no protest, he planted himself backwards in a chair and grinned. 'What do you want out of life, Zelle?' he asked with his arms astride the back of the chair and his chin resting on his arms.

'Mr. Sims, why ever do you ask me such a question?' she answered his question with a question. 'You should be helping me with these dishes instead of fooling around. I don't want to be in this kitchen all night.'

Looking up into her beautiful but angry face, his eyes sparkled and he could barely contain himself. 'Just wondering what you dream about.'

'I don't dream too much about anything. I work too hard to dream.' Her words were clearly shaped by irritation.

'Surely you want something out of life more than what you already got,' he persisted.

'I want a better school for my students. I want an easier time for black folks, that's what I want.'

'I'm talkin' about for yourself. What you want for yourself?'

Zelle lived in a world where helping others came as naturally as breathing. She wanted to be happy and helping others made her happy. She didn't know how to answer Charles' question so she said, 'There's nothing I want for myself.'

'Been thinkin' a lot about us,' he said, realizing she wasn't going to go in the direction he was steering.

Zelle stopped drying the plate in her hands and looked into Charles' face. In the warmth of his eyes, she saw the man she had come to love with all her heart. *Us* was a word she thought about during most of her waking moments, but to hear it from Charles' lips was terrifying.

'What about us,' she asked cautiously.

'Been thinkin' that if I went to work at the railroad yard, I could maybe support a wife. Steady work and all.'

Little tendrils of nerve fibers crawled up the side of Zelle's neck and face. It was the same sensation she felt the first time she looked into Charles' eyes at the Juneteenth picnic, a mixture of pleasure and embarrassment. She had always prayed that someday Charles might propose but, as time went by, she had started losing hope. He was such a handsome man, what could he possibly want with her?

'And why do you need to support a wife, Mr. Sims?' she asked, afraid to assume too much.

'I've had my eye on this beautiful young lady for some time and I want to marry her.'

'Do I know her?' she asked timidly.

'Zelle Marshall, I'm asking you to marry me and you know it.'

Charles suddenly pulled the dishtowel out of her hand and drew her to his lap.

'You mean everything to me and you are the person I want to spend my life with. I love you.'

He kissed her on the lips for the very first time. Zelle pulled back. 'Mama or Papa might come,' she said with alarm. 'Or worse, Ivy.'

'I love you, Zelle,' he repeated. 'Do you love me?'

'Yes, I do,' she replied, finally saying out loud what she had been hiding inside her heart.

'Then it's okay if I ask your Papa for your hand?'

'Yes," she said, overcome with joy.

For Christmas Charles gave Zelle a gold ring with a tiny opal setting, Zelle's birthstone. Mama and Papa were pleased about the upcoming marriage, her sister Ivy was thrilled at the prospect of being a bridesmaid and her baby brother, Jeremiah, wanted to be a bridesmaid, too.

'Boys can't be bridesmaids, Jeremiah,' she laughed. 'How would you like to be the ring bearer?'

'Yay, yay, I get to be ring bearer,' Jeremiah chirped gleefully. His delight mirrored the mood of the entire family.

'When are you two going to set the date?' Sarah Marshall asked.

'How about June?' Zelle whispered to Charles, leaning in to his body with a closeness she had never shown in front of her family.

'June it is,' her Papa said proudly.

Winter hovered as though spring was never going to arrive and the frigid days of January and February locked everyone into a pattern of seeking warmth and staying put. Charles hired on at the railroad yard and didn't see much of

Hollis anymore. He also stopped going to the Maple Leaf Club and tried to put Ophelia Lucas out of his thoughts.

When March offered the promise of more temperate weather, a cold front moved in on Charles that sent him to his knees begging for mercy. Ophelia Lucas announced to him that she was having his child.

'I've missed you, Charles,' she said as he stood opposite her in the dress shop, summoned by Hollis to go see her because she wasn't doing well.

'I couldn't see you, Ophelia. I told you I was seein' a young lady,' Charles said defensively.

'And she's better than me?' Ophelia spat the words at him.

'No, but I'm in love with her, not you.'

'You should have thought of that before you made love to me.'

'You know I didn't mean for that to happen. It was a mistake and I've regretted it ever since.'

'You're a cold man, Charleston Sims. Not a drop of warmth runs in your blood.'

Charles looked at Ophelia, thinking, 'get on with it and let me go,' but he said nothing.

'Well, I'm afraid I have bad news for you, given how much you regret...'

'What are you talkin' about?' he interrupted.

'I'm having your baby,' she said with less hostility.

'Are you sure it's mine?'

The hostility returned in a flash. 'You're cold, Charles, don't be a bastard, too. I haven't been with anyone else since I been in Sedalia.'

Charles waved his arms in the air in a gesture of futility. 'What do you expect me to do?'

'The right thing, of course. That is, if you even know what the right thing is.'

'Did you know what the right thing was when you seduced me after I told you I was seein' someone else?'

With that, Charles turned and left the shop all in one swift motion disappearing into the night like he had never been there. He erased Ophelia from his mind and heart and thought he could get back to his life with Zelle unfettered.

20 Rumors or Truth

"When you're engaged to such a handsome man, there's bound to be those who think it can't last. Folks can say such mean things and not bat an eye. They say things to you not even your worst enemies would dare to say.

"It started at the school when the other teachers hinted I better keep a close eye on my fiancée. Then there were whispers at the market and finally folks at church started giving me a funny eye when they saw me with Charles on Sunday. I didn't pay it any mind; I just figured they were jealous, thought I wasn't pretty enough for Charles. I thought they'd leave me alone once we were married.

"Then one Sunday after church, Charles came to me as I was putting away the organ music. There was desperation in his eyes and panic in his voice. I pretended to be busy because I didn't want to talk to him at just that moment. There had been so many rumors and I needed more time to figure out what it all meant before I asked if they were true. Surely they were not...

"He grabbed me by the shoulders and there were tears in his eyes.

'I have to talk to you,' he said frantically.

'You're scaring me,' I told him and I tried to pull away from his grip.

"But he wouldn't let me go.

'Please forgive me, Zelle,' he begged.

"I had never seen Charles cry and could not imagine what would make him do so.

'Zelle,' he finally said, 'Ophelia Lucas is going to have a baby.'

'Who is Ophelia Lucas?' I asked, trying to breathe.

'She's Hollis' cousin.'

'Is it yours?' I asked indignantly.

'It was an accident,' he sobbed.

"I remember where I was sitting and what dress I had on and what scent I had used after my bath. And here was this sudden stranger on his knees crying in my lap, telling me that another woman was carrying his child."

'I talked to your Papa,' he said. 'He made me see that God is a God of forgiveness.'

'You told Papa?' I asked in surprise, my voice cracking in anguish.

'I didn't know who else to turn to.' Charles touched my shoulder. 'Please, give me a second chance.'

"Later, Papa told me I should forgive Charles. He told me that all God's children make mistakes and we must not let Charles' mistake ruin him.

'What would you have me do?' I asked.

'Let the wedding go on as planned.'

'I can't, Papa. I can't.'

'Folks will stop talking when they see there's nothing to talk about.'

I pause because the memory is so painful. What I remember feeling then was that Papa loved Charles more than he loved me or he could not have asked me to do such a thing. I remember feeling betrayed and rejected but I didn't dwell on that feeling then and I cannot dwell on it now. I have a ways to go to get to the thing I want Neely to know and I draw on everything in me to continue.

"Everything beautiful can turn ugly so quickly and sometimes there is not even time to think before it happens. A big black hole opens up and swallows you whole and closes up again and then life goes on. Only nobody notices that you've been swallowed up in a black hole. That's what hurts the most, I think--the fact that nobody notices--and from somewhere inside the invisible hole, you must carry on as though nothing has happened.

"That night I slipped the gold ring off my finger and put it in my jewelry box, vowing never to wear it again. The Black Hole had swallowed me alive."

21 Neely

Ganzie's heartache rips right through me like a lightning strike. I feel her pain as if it's my own and I start crying.

She reaches out and touches my shoulder.

"Don't be upset, Neely."

I can't be consoled. "The great romance I thought you had with Grandpa Charles, it was nothing but a sham. He wasn't worth the time you took to love him."

"He was a man, baby, nothing but a man."

"He was a bastard."

"Don't judge him so harshly. All men have shortcomings."

I get up and walk to the window not sure I want to hear any more about Grandpa Charles. All men have shortcomings for sure but that was no excuse. What if Gill was like all the rest? How could I know? How would I survive if he were no better than the rest?

Ganzie struggles to rise from her seat and joins me at the window. Putting her fragile arms around my waist, she says, "Come back and sit down. The story's not over yet. When it is, you'll understand your Grandpa more."

She moves the closed photo album to the floor and says, "Charles convinced Papa that he had been under the temptation of the devil himself and he swore to never bring shame on the family again. It was not an easy task. Papa prayed on it for weeks but in the end, he asked me to forgive Charles.

"Papa performed the wedding ceremony. I had a beautiful hand-made white lace dress and Mama bought me white combs for my hair and gave me her white pearls to wear. After we were married, Charles really tried to make me happy and I believed he would keep his word. It made forgiving him easier."

22 The Secret Begins

From the beginning, the life Charles shared with Zelle was the life he really wanted and he did everything in his power to make her forgive and forget. He showed extreme patience and abundant tenderness for his new bride and eventually was able to overcome her reluctance for intimacy. 'I love *you*, no one else but you,' he repeated over and over, until she believed it and forgot all about the fact he had performed the same ritual with Ophelia Lucas. Eventually he could touch her without bringing to her mind the image of his hand touching Ophelia in the same place.

In time Charleston Sims was able to live his life without dwelling in constant repentance. In time he came to know the depths of Zelle's forgiveness, but as the summer of 1907 shifted into fall and the nights turned cool from imperceptibly shorter days, he was brought face to face with his own Achilles' heart.

He hadn't seen much of Hollis McAdoo since the circumstance of Ophelia's pregnancy all but severed ties between the boyhood pals. So no one was more surprised than Charles when Hollis accosted him outside the railroad yards on a hot, humid September afternoon.

'Phelia had the baby,' Hollis said forthrightly without so much as a salutation.

Charles looked into the face of his old friend but said nothing.

'What you gonna do, man?' Hollis insisted.

'There's nothin' I can do, Hollis, and you know it. It was not my fault.'

'Aw, shit, weren't your fault? Whose fault you think it were? She sure didn't make that baby by herself.'

'You don't know anything about it.'

'I know'd she thought somethin' was more'n what it was, but she ain't no bad lady. Go an' see her, Charles. She been havin' a real hard time. Just go see her and then you can let it be.'

For days Charles mulled over what Hollis had said. The more he tried not to think about it, the more it was on his mind.

Go and see her, Hollis had urged.

Unthinkable, Charles concluded. He had promised Zelle he would never see Ophelia again and he didn't want to go back on his word.

But finally his curiosity got the best of him and a desire to clear his conscience got too great to ignore. On a day when the clouds were low in the sky and a constant drizzle permeated the air, he crept into the shop on Broadway as unobtrusively as possible knowing he couldn't stay long.

Ophelia was sitting beside a small cradle at the back of the room. When she looked up to see it was not another customer but rather Charleston Sims, she didn't move from her position. Her back, however, stiffened and the expression on her face clouded over with animosity.

'What do you want, Charles,' she asked brusquely.

'Hollis told me you had the baby. I came to see how you were farin'.' He tried to move closer but was stopped by her icy glare.

'I'm managing,' was all she said.

'I see you're back at work.'

'Charles,' she steered the conversation on a more direct course, 'I don't want anything from you.'

'That's good, because I got nothin' for you,' he responded sharply.

Ophelia raised her voice. 'Then go, get out!'

Charles turned to leave but was stopped by the sound of a baby gurgling and whimpering.

'Can I see it?' he asked in a more conciliatory tone.

'What for?' she snapped, not willing to make it easy.

'Just let me see the baby, Ophelia. Then I'll go and not bother you anymore.'

She looked at Charles strangely. He was certainly not the man she thought he was when they met at the Maple Leaf Club. The Charles she fell in love with was a different person—shy, handsome, unaware of his charm, interested in her every word. But this Charles was cold and distant and suddenly not worth the energy of her anger and resentment.

She picked up the baby and offered it to him. At first he held back, but she encouraged him. 'Go ahead. Take her,' she said. 'It's a girl.'

Charles held the tiny bundle awkwardly. He wasn't sure what to do, but was soon captivated by the minuscule creature who fit into the palms of his two hands. Her skin was fair like his and her hair jet black and curly. Fingers like prongs extended from her hands, each one waving jerkily through the air. The baby stopped whimpering and settled back into a sleeping state.

'She's beautiful,' Charles sighed.

'I named her after my mother,' Ophelia said.

'I didn't mean for this to happen, Ophelia. You must believe me.'

'Yes, I believe you, but I'm not sorry it did. I wouldn't give up this baby for anything.'

'People will be cruel to her because she doesn't have a father.'

'Oh, she has a father all right. You mean because I don't have a husband. Go ahead and say it.'

'It's one and the same, isn't it?'

'It doesn't matter. She's here and I'll take care of her the best I can.'

'I wish I could help you some.'

'You made your decision when you married Zelle. Given the kind of man you are, I suspect it was the right thing for you to do. Don't worry about us, we'll be fine.'

Charles held the baby gingerly and rocked her in his arms. He was filled with an abundance of emotions that made him question who he was and why he was put on this earth. He was an orphan, a terrified young boy, a brother, an uncle, a proud man, a carpenter, a railroad laborer, a man of faith, an errant lover, a son-in-law, a husband...and now a father. He was all these things and yet he was nothing.

Now a new purpose had emerged. He couldn't be any good to anybody if he closed his eyes to the small baby in his arms. He held her tiny fingers in his hand and kissed them one by one. In that instant, his heart opened up and made a place for the child he couldn't claim as his own.

23 Neely

I feel a strange connection to the world of Turn-of-the-Century Sedalia, Missouri and life without the benefit of modern conveniences. Everything was new—cars, telephones, electricity. Yet the troubles Ganzie faced were as old as history. My problems are not unique and it's selfish of me to think they are.

She was strong yet so vulnerable, full of hope yet living with restraint and restriction, having the courage to believe in love yet finding it soiled and tarnished. It made me realize she and I aren't so different.

How would I have reacted if those things had happened to me? Could I have married Roland if he had fathered a child by another woman? Could I have ever forgiven him, not only for the rest of the world to see, but inside my damaged heart where it mattered? Each day, could I look at him with non-accusing eyes and each night could I let him touch me, make love to me? The questions have no answers and I am overwhelmed with sadness.

"I hope you don't mind me rambling on so," Ganzie says.

"I had no idea that your life wasn't perfect."

"Nobody's life is perfect. All we can do is figure it out the best we can and then keep moving on."

"Well, it looks like you got it figured out and I guess it's up to me to do the same."

Ganzie doesn't reply and I don't know what else to say. I lean over and kiss her forehead and am filled with love and admiration for the woman she was and the woman she has become.

"I'm so glad you're here," she says.

"Me too."

"I want you to know how much I love you and if I tell you things that hurt, that's not my intention. It's my hope that they will help you heal and that, before you leave, you'll know the right thing to do."

I am totally confused by her words and the look on her face, a mixture of anguish and resolve and it's my turn to say nothing.

I can tell she's tired but she continues as if on a mission.

"Your Grandpa Charles was a good man but things weren't always good between us."

"I thought you forgave him."

"Yes, I forgave him but I don't think he ever forgave himself. He worked long hours, saved money and built this house as part of his penance, I think. I thought it was kind of silly, but he had more foresight than I did as if he knew that someday it would be all I had to show for our life together."

"But you had Mama. She represents your life together."

"Now, that's the story I need to tell you about. Things happened that never got explained and I think it's time you know the truth."

"What truth?" I ask with apprehension.

Ganzie, almost in a trance, continues the saga of Charleston Sims. "Five years went by and our life was good. The only thing missing was a child. For a time, I feared God was punishing me for taking Charles away from his true responsibility. My selfishness, I was sure, had not gone unnoticed."

I listen intently and then see soft tears moistening Ganzie's eyes. I am afraid to hear what is about to come.

"In the early winter of 1912 lots of folks got sick with pneumonia and died. It took the elderly and it took the young. And it took Ophelia Lucas. When she became ill, there was never any hope she would recover."

24 Living with Regret

Part of Charles' need for constant forgiveness was because he was constantly doing things he needed to be forgiven for. Secretly he had, from the beginning, maintained contact with Ophelia in order to see the baby. Then, as the child grew, his visits were more frequent.

'Papa,' she called him when he came to visit, running to greet him and jumping into his arms. Charles loved the exuberance of the youngster who looked so much like him and his heart leapt with joy. When he could, he gave Ophelia money to help care for their daughter but mostly he stopped by just to see her, hold her and read to her. With her, he felt a completeness that drew him back time and time again.

'She's got your eyes, Charles,' Ophelia said on an early visit.

'I know she's mine, Ophelia. I'm not denyin' it.'

'No, it's just me you're denying.'

'I'm not gonna fight with you. You knew all along what you were gettin' into.'

'I'll never know how you can be such a good father and such a rotten man, Charles. I'm glad I never got close enough to you to need you for anything.'

'I have nothin' to give you. I'm married now and I plan to stay that way.'

'I don't want you, Charleston Sims. If it weren't for our daughter, I wouldn't even let you in the door.'

'Thank you for not keepin' me away, I couldn't live without her.'

'Neither could I.'

It would have crushed Zelle to know that Charles had a secret life with Ophelia but it was not his intention to hurt her; he just needed to be with his daughter. Unfortunately, that meant he also spent time with the mother.

'Could you to stay for supper?' she asked one night.

'I don't want to get in your way.'

'It's not for me, Charles, it's for the child. Honestly, I don't know how you can be so vain. They always say good looking men are vain so I guess that's your problem.'

'I'm not vain, Ophelia. I'm just a man who made a mistake and I'm doin' the best I can to make it right.'

But even Charles was unsure of what the mistake was—having a baby by a woman other than his fiancée or marrying his fiancée instead of the mother of his child.

Over dinner, they were almost like a family and Charles felt an unfamiliar pang in his heart. He and Zelle had no children and it didn't look like they would ever be blessed with one. He found himself looking at Ophelia and trying to find Zelle's face. One night, he almost kissed Ophelia and then he knew he was going too far in his attempt to make things right.

'I didn't mean to hurt you, Ophelia,' he said sincerely.

'I know you didn't, Charles. It just happened. But look what we accomplished. Just one silly night and look at this beautiful child. I'd do it all over again if given the chance.'

Yes, his daughter was worth the trouble that her being caused. And his relationship with Ophelia had grown into an unexpected friendship. So it was completely natural for her to turn to him in her time of need. As usual, she didn't mince words.

'I want you and Zelle to raise my baby.'

'I can't do that, Ophelia, and you know it.'

'I got no family to speak of and I don't want her to be brought up by strangers. If you love her as much as you say, you'll take her and keep her safe."

'Ophelia, don't ask this of me.'

'I'm dying, Charles. Got no more to give. It's your turn. Please take Alma and see to it she has a good life.'

25 Neely

Alma! For a few seconds I can't breathe. Alma is my mother! But if Alma is Ophelia's daughter that means Ganzie is not my grandmother. Everything I have ever believed in suddenly collapses. I stare hard into Ganzie's eyes looking for a sign I misunderstood but all I see is a plea for understanding.

"Maybe I shouldn't have told you about Ophelia Lucas but this secret has been festering for too long and now's the time to get it out in the open. As a matter of fact, now is the only time."

Sometimes when I pass someone on the street or in the grocery store, I wonder what it takes for a stranger to become an acquaintance, an acquaintance to become a friend and a friend to turn into someone you love. I never imagined it could go the other way but Ganzie has suddenly become a stranger, someone I've never seen before and will probably never see again. Her wrinkled face is unfamiliar; her once dark eyes don't connect with mine. I always thought I looked like her; now I am disappearing because I don't have any idea who I am.

When I can finally form words out of all the confusion in my head, all I can say is, "What are you trying to tell me?"

"Your mama is the daughter of Charles and Ophelia. I never had any children of my own."

"Oh God...," I choke.

"The day Charles came to me and told me that Ophelia was dying and he wanted to bring his daughter into our home, I thought I was being punished again.

'Zelle,' he said, 'she has no one else to care for her. The least I can do is give her a home. She is, after all, my flesh and blood.'

"I could tell it was something he wanted very badly and I didn't have the heart to say no.

"When I first saw the little girl, she wasn't much to look at—her hair hadn't been combed and her nose was running. I didn't know anything about being a mother, but I knew she needed a bath. Then I combed her hair and dressed her in the new outfit Charles had bought for her. We ate supper like a family and at bedtime, your Grandpa and I tucked her in together. When she started crying, Charles held her in his arms until she stopped. It was obvious she knew her Papa and I realized how many times he had lied to me about where he was going when he left home."

Ganzie's face is clouded with sadness and regret and she adds, "I was never going to have a child of my own. The least I could do was take good care of Alma."

"Why did you keep it a secret?" I ask, still trying to recover from my astonishment.

"It wasn't a secret. We just didn't talk about it."

"But everybody knew..."

"Yes, everybody knew but after awhile they acted like they forgot so we didn't talk about it anymore."

"You must have hated Grandpa."

"No, not hated."

"But he lied to you and he hurt you."

"If we only loved the people who didn't hurt us, there wouldn't be much love in the world. I forgave your Grandpa long before he forgave himself. I wish you had known him. Then maybe you'd understand.

"You're not my grandmother," I say barely above a whisper.

"I'm your grandmother in all the ways that matter."

"Nothing matters anymore."

"Don't say that, Neely!"

"Why are you telling me this?"

"In all of us are the roots of where we came from as well as how we were raised. You've been affected by both and you need a chance to figure yourself out so you don't keep drifting through life, unsure and afraid."

"And this will help?"

"It has the power to heal if you let it."

"There's so much about people we never know," I sigh. "They move in and out of your life and you can only scratch the surface of who they are. Now I realize not only do I not know myself, I don't know you."

"That's my point exactly."

"Mama knows, doesn't she?"

"If she has any memory of her real mother, she's never said. I don't suppose she would have told me even if she did. We don't talk much."

I don't know what to say. My world is upside down and I don't think it'll ever be upright again. But one thing for sure: the problems I came to Sedalia with are insignificant compared to this.

I am trying not to cry because it seems such a babyish thing to do. I have to be strong because I no longer have anybody to turn to.

"Listen, I didn't tell you any of this to hurt you. I won't be around much longer and there was no one else to tell you."

I suddenly realize what she's saying. "How sick are you, Ganzie?" I ask.

"Pretty sick, but please don't worry about me. God has given me a long life and I'm grateful."

"What do you want me to do?"

"Forgive me," Ganzie replies simply.

"I have nothing to forgive you for."

"Every time I looked into your mother's face, all I could see was the face of Ophelia Lucas. It caused a wound that has never healed. To this day. You think your Mama is hard to love? Well it may be more my fault than hers. "

"Oh, Ganzie," I groan.

"It's important that you know who you are and where you came from. It doesn't change a thing; it just helps explain things."

"How can you love me the way you say you do?"

"All I can say is that God truly works in mysterious ways. If I could have loved that little girl half as much as I love you..., well, what can I say? You were the sweetest child. Why, you even gave me my name."

"I don't know what to say."

"There's nothing you need to say. I just couldn't take it to the grave with me."

"Don't talk like that."

"Someday I want you to talk to your Mama about it. It may settle things between you."

"I can't imagine how I'd bring it up."

"Just think about it and maybe the right time will present itself."

26 Ganzie

The afternoon drifted by and the entire day fades into evening. I am very tired but I am not yet at the end of my journey. Putting memories into words has filled me with melancholy. Telling Neely about Charleston Sims reminds me that love has many unexpected faces.

In time I found happiness with my family. In time I accepted the past and looked forward to the future. But in 1915 when Joe Spencer came to town, I was suffering and thought I'd never recover. Now I want to tell Neely about Joe Spencer and I won't be able to rest until I do.

After a light supper of vegetable soup and saltine crackers has been fixed and eaten, I continue in spite of my fatigue.

"I owe you an apology. You came here with one problem and I've given you another in its place."

Neely waves her hand in dismissal.

"But I haven't forgotten about you and Gill," I insist.

"He's not important now."

"He's very important. And when you get back home, you've got to face up to it." I touch her hand and pat it gently.

"You probably think this old woman can't possibly understand how you feel, but I do."

"I am so confused right now I can't think."

"You're strong, Neely, stronger than you know. You'll sort this out and you'll do the right thing. And when you're trying to decide what the right thing is, I want you to remember a story about a man named Joe Spencer.

"By 1915, I had been married eight years and had an eight-year-old step-daughter who I tried real hard to love. Your Grandpa continued to work long hours to provide for us while my teaching duties included a night class in sewing and needlework at Smith College. We saw little of each other during the week and Sundays were very important, just like they had been when your Grandpa was courting me.

"Going to church was the highlight of the day. For the most part, we were able to hold our heads high and worship the Lord without the taint of human judgment. Then, like as not, we'd have dinner with Mama and Papa. Ivy had taken off for St. Louis to go to school and never came back. And Jeremiah was going through a rebellious period. Papa was having a real hard time handling him and sometimes turned to your Grandpa for help."

Neely interrupts. "I'm surprised your Papa thought so highly of him."

"I don't think Papa ever thought any less of Charles. I think he admired him for having the courage to take care of his own in spite of what other people might say. But Jeremiah wasn't blessed with the same level of understanding of the human condition and he thought Papa a fool. That might have been Papa's mistake with his son--encouraging him to listen to a man whose own reputation had been sullied."

"You've never talked about Jeremiah."

"He got in with a bad crowd in Kansas City and was killed in a barroom brawl when he was only nineteen. It nearly broke Papa's spirit and we didn't talk about him much after that.

"The very next year Papa himself was killed in an automobile accident on his way to St. Louis to see Ivy. It was his first car and he wasn't much of a driver. Those were sad times, indeed."

This is not the story I want to tell and I need to stay on track or I'll never have enough energy to get to the end. With a renewed strength from an unknown source, I continue.

"Charles and I rarely talked about anything other than the business of the day. I was not unhappy, but I no longer felt like Charleston Sims was the beginning and end of my day. I don't recall actually being angry with him but I'm not sure I had forgiven him. Every day I struggled with feelings I didn't understand.

"When Joe Spencer came to town, life caught me off guard and showed me, no matter how many forks you come to in the road, you can only travel one. To try to do otherwise freezes you on the spot. God gives us little tests from time to time to measure our strength and wisdom. One of my tests was Joe Spencer. He was a fork in the road that could have taken me down a very different path."

Thinking of Joe Spencer still gives me the chills. My voice takes on a quality of extraordinary remembrance, a restoration of lost cells and echoes from the past. I say, almost reverently, "I fell in love with Joe Spencer. Maybe it was enough to last a lifetime, but I didn't know for sure so I stayed with Charles. He needed me and so did his daughter."

I glance at Neely and see that she's lost in confusion by the story I've been telling. I know it's a long and rambling tale and I should get to the point as quickly as possible. But what is the point? Am I merely trying to absolve my guilt about the lies I helped perpetuate or am I trying to help her solve her own puzzlement? Nothing I'm saying is very helpful, I know. Yet I must persist. Somewhere in the labyrinth that was my life, I'm hoping she'll find the key to hers.

"Joe was born in Virginia," I continue, "and educated at Wilberforce, Ohio, and he was a new breed of colored man who did not limit his ambitions to working in the trades. He was an intellectual who favored the works of W.E.B. DuBois and had studied English literature and history and politics. Papa wouldn't have liked Joe much and it was truly unusual for me to like someone Papa wouldn't like. But it was more unusual for me to like someone who didn't share my views.

"My friendship with Joe had a rather ordinary beginning. He stopped by my classroom because he saw the light still on after evening classes were supposed to be over. It was just that simple. A light on when it wasn't supposed to be and then someone new walks into your life who isn't supposed to be there and changes it forever.

"But let me tell you one thing, I'm not sorry about letting Joe Spencer into my life. Every woman, if she's lucky, knows a Joe Spencer."

27 The Ballad of Joe Spencer

'Excuse me,' Joe Spencer said when he found someone in a room he expected to be empty. Startled, Zelle looked up from where she stood at the sewing table putting away some fabric and patterns. 'I'm sorry,' he apologized, 'I thought everyone had gone home.'

When she realized she had nothing to fear from the stranger, Zelle relaxed and responded easily, 'As you can see, I'm still here, but I'm on my way out.'

'I didn't mean to intrude.' He turned to leave and then turned back, somehow drawn to bridge the natural gap between two strangers. 'My name is Joe Spencer,' he volunteered. 'I'm the new English teacher.'

Zelle, in her usual forthright manner smiled and replied, 'Pleased to meet you, Mr. Spencer. I'm Zelle Sims. As you might guess, I teach sewing and needlework. Just two nights a week though. In the daytime I teach at the elementary school.'

'That must keep you pretty busy.'

'I love to keep busy.'

'It makes all the difference,' he said sagely, 'if you love your work.'

The newcomer's appearance caught her attention immediately. His tall frame was clad impeccably in a lightweight gray gabardine suit complete with white shirt and tie and his black brogues were well-polished. Smooth brown skin like chocolate soufflé covered his face and hands and eyes like pools of liquid coal dominated his features. As thoroughly captivating as his looks were, however, it was his voice that caused a comment.

'You're not from around here, are you?' she asked.

'No, Ma'am. I was born in Virginia but taught school in Chicago. Lost most of my accent there.'

'Chicago, now that's a big place. What on earth brings you to Sedalia?'

'Chicago is getting to be kind of a rough town and I took the first job offered so I could get out.'

'This is a fine school. I hope it'll live up to your expectations.'

'So far everything is to my liking.'

'I'm glad to hear it, Mr. Spencer. Now, I'm on my way out. It was mighty nice meeting you.'

'Can I give you a ride home?' he asked politely.

'You have an automobile?' Zelle asked in astonishment.

'One of the luxuries of hard work and no responsibilities.'

'I appreciate the offer, but my husband might not think too kindly of another gentleman bringing me home.'

'Oh, you're married,' he said with obvious disappointment in his voice. 'I apologize for my impertinence.'

'I take it as a kindness and I appreciate it.' A slight embarrassment flushed Zelle's cheeks and she raised her hand to shield her face from his view.

'I hope you have a safe way home.'

'I usually walk. It's not far.'

'If you ever need a ride, don't hesitate to ask.'

'I won't, Mr. Spencer, and thank you.'

'Call me Joe. Mr. Spencer makes me feel like my father and I've got a long way to go to be the man he was.'

'Good night, then, Joe. Maybe I'll see you again sometime.'

Zelle didn't have any intention of allowing a relationship to develop between her and Joe Spencer. However, on the days she taught, Joe took to dropping by the Home Arts Room at the end of the evening. Zelle would stop what she was doing, smile at him warmly and give him her full attention. At first they only talked about the trivialities of the day, but soon their conversation expanded to include a range of important issues and feelings.

'Colored people are swarming into northern cities,' Joe told her one night. 'There are no jobs in the south and the north feels like Utopia, but the truth is there are no Utopias. The northern whites resent the influx of Negroes and the northern Negroes feel their life is being diminished by their southern brothers. That's part of the reason I left Chicago. Too many black folks and too much poverty. And too many poor black folks who don't like other black folks who are trying to do better. It makes it tough for everybody.'

'I've been so sheltered,' Zelle answered. 'Nothing in my life in Sedalia has prepared me for what it's like out in the real world. Papa worked hard to provide his family with a shield from racial ugliness. I don't think I could live anywhere else.'

'Don't be ashamed. There's no grace from God for suffering the way some folks suffer. My father was a sharecropper and it's a miracle that I've been able to travel down a different road. I know how lucky I am and I wouldn't trade it for anything.'

'I'm not ashamed. I know how lucky I am, too.'

'That's good. Feel lucky and then let it go.'

'What do you mean, let it go?'

'Just live your life as naturally as you can. There are plenty of forces in the world to remind you that you're colored and you can't do what everyone else can do. So you live your life as naturally as you can and hope the bad things never catch up with you.'

'Papa told me Booker T. Washington died,' Zelle told Joe on one night.

'I know, I heard,' Joe said flatly.

'You didn't think too much of him, did you?'

'You've heard of a man ahead of his time? Well, he was a man behind his time. He was a good man but he didn't want enough for black folks.'

'Maybe he just wanted to keep us alive until something better came along.'

'And where was it going to come from? Nobody gives you anything in life. You have to reach out and take it.'

Joe moved his fist through the air in a forceful motion causing Zelle to shrink away from him. 'You scare me when you say those things.'

'No need to be afraid, Zelle, but you must remember what I said. Nobody gives you anything in life.' And then he curled his fingers as though he was grabbing something out of the air. He was such a strong man and his confident manner caught Zelle in its vise and held her fast.

Their brief meetings began to occupy more of an evening and sometimes she was later getting home than usual. Charles was usually asleep in his chair and Alma safely tucked in bed so she hardly felt missed. So it was a lonely Zelle who went to bed on such nights trapped in a world not of her making, holding close to her the intense feelings that had been liberated by the company of another man. Her body would ache to be held and caressed and her heart would cry out for love. When sleep finally released her from the distress of her everyday existence, her dreams would take her to a place of beauty where Joe and not Charles was the man resting peacefully at her side.

As the months went by and the visits continued, Zelle realized she was being courted much in the same way she was when Charles showed up at church every Sunday. She didn't encourage Joe Spencer, neither did she discourage him. Lightness inflated her heart when he was around that made her feel young and beautiful again. The echo of his footsteps in the hallway and the sound of his voice when he entered her room caused her heart to leap. Their conversations fed her soul.

However, she never had any intention of following her feelings into action so no one was more surprised than she when Joe kissed her for the very first time. It happened one night when they had known each other about six months and a February winter night raged outside making the inside warmth cozy and appealing.

'I can't let you walk home tonight, Zelle,' he said. 'It's freezing out.'

'You know I can't ride in your automobile, Joe. I could never explain it to Mr. Sims.'

'If your husband cared about you at all, he wouldn't let you walk home after dark on a winter night, or any night for that matter.'

'You don't know what you're talking about. He works long hours, too, and he watches out for his little girl on the nights I teach.'

'His little girl?'

Zelle had not meant to say those words and lowered her eyes quickly. Then desperately needing to share her pain, she told Joe her secret. Without hesitation, she revealed the story of how Alma came into her life. When she finished, he moved close to her and said, 'You've suffered much, Zelle Sims, don't ever think you haven't.'

'But it's not the kind of suffering that makes the difference between life and death, so it doesn't count.'

'It depends on who's keeping score. I think it counts.'

He put his hands to her face without thinking and then bent down to kiss her first on the forehead and then his lips moved to her cheek and then rested on her mouth. Zelle was too shocked to move away from him and as his lips lingered, she felt a response welling up inside her. She felt her own lips accept the pressure of his and then return the kiss. Then frightened by her emotions, she quickly pulled away.

'You mustn't do that,' she stammered.

'I'm sorry, Zelle.'

'It's not your fault.'

'It's all my fault.' And then without thinking about what he was doing, he grabbed her shoulders and kissed her again. 'I love you,' he said softly into her ear, defining his feelings by the only words he knew.

Zelle pulled from his grasp and turned her back to him. 'Don't say that,' she said crisply.

'I know I shouldn't but it's as true as anything I've ever known. If you have any feelings for me, you must tell me.'

'We've been fooling around with our destinies, Joe. This wasn't meant to happen. I have a husband and a child. No matter what I feel, I cannot think of you in this way.'

'I think our destinies have been fooling around with us. They put us in the same slot of time and space and then expected us to stay away from each other.' He walked around to stand in front of her again and asked, 'Do you love me, Zelle?'

She looked into the coals of his eyes and saw feelings she couldn't deny. She spoke words as close to that truth as she could express. 'I don't know what love is. I fell in what I thought was love with the first man who courted me and married him without ever really knowing who he was. We've tried to build a life together and it's the only life I know. Now you come into my world and bring with you feelings I never imagined existed. It's very confusing for me.'

'I will make it simple for you. Tell me you love me. I need to know if it's possible.'

'If holding you dear in my heart is love, I love you. If desiring your safety above all else is love, I love you. If wanting to be with you all the time is love, then, yes, I love you.'

Joe kissed Zelle again and the room spiraled around them for a brief moment and then it was over. Tears formed in the corners of her eyes and Zelle lamented in a weak voice, 'What's going to become of us now?'

Joe wrapped her in his arms and held her close. In the circle of his grip he tried to shut out the rest of the world and keep them both safe from harm.

28 Neely

Ganzie's voice is weak with exhaustion when she says, "It's late, Neely. I think it's time for me to go to bed." The words are barely above a whisper.

"But, Ganzie," I insist, "you must tell me what happened."

Ganzie waves her hand and smiles. "Actually, nothing happened," she says. "I couldn't bring myself to leave Charles and Joe left Sedalia at the end of the spring term. For him, the choice was clear--if he couldn't have me, he had to leave. For me, it was much more difficult. I loved him, but I couldn't do anything about it. There had already been enough scandal in my life. I never saw him again.

"I wanted to be with Joe but I also wanted to stay with Charles. But as I said, if you try to go down two paths at the same time, you get frozen on the spot. I couldn't make a decision so Joe made it for me by leaving. I think he did the best thing for both of us."

"And you have no regrets?" I ask.

"We all make choices and then wonder 'what if' about what we didn't choose."

"But you didn't make a choice, you just let him go away."

"I didn't just *let* him go away, I couldn't *stop* him from leaving. Neither could I ask him to stay. It was the choice of indecision and it was all I could do at the time."

"But you loved Joe, didn't you?" I prod.

"Yes, I loved him but those were childish feelings. My life was not based on such whimsy. And after all is said and done, I don't regret staying with your Grandpa. Maybe we weren't meant to be together, maybe he should have married Ophelia and maybe they should have raised their daughter, but those are all just maybes."

Ganzie lowers her head. "Joe wasn't the kind of man who could stay in one place for very long. He would have left eventually anyway."

"Are you telling me I should stay with Roland?"

"In my day people made those kinds of decisions based on what other people would say or think. You didn't always have a personal choice."

"Times aren't so different now."

"That may be true but no matter what anybody says, the most important thing is for you to be able to look at yourself in the mirror every morning without flinching."

"You're telling me to forget about Gill, aren't you?"

"I'm telling you that you have to decide what's best for you and then do it. That's the only way you can live with yourself."

29 Facing Reality

It's clear that Ganzie is too tired to talk any longer. She almost dozes off where she sits and I lift her thin body from the couch and help her to bed. For quite a long time, I watch her sleeping, worrying that something bad will happen if I leave the room. But then I can't bear the silence and the aloneness and I go back to the living room, pick up the phone, and dial Gill's number.

I almost put the receiver back in its cradle, but when I hear his soft "hello," I'm glad I called.

"It's me, Gill," I say. "I know it's late but I had to call."

"Is everything okay?" he asks with concern. "What's going on?"

"I'm visiting my grandmother."

"That's what Erica said. Is everything okay?" he repeats more forcefully.

"She's dying."

"I'm so sorry. Is there anything I can do?"

"Not right now." I take a deep breath and then decide to plunge into the abyss. "Gill, there's something I need to tell you."

"What is it, Babe?"

"Roland hit me Sunday night."

"That son of a bitch," he mutters angrily.

"It wasn't all his fault. I said some pretty awful things."

"That's no excuse. Don't defend that prick."

No excuse but surely reasons. I had done everything but raise his hand and swing it across my face.

"There's more..." I hesitate but know I can't keep it from Gill, actually don't want to keep it from him. "He threatened to kill me if he found out I was sleeping with someone else."

"Jeezus."

"I don't think he meant it but I wanted to put some distance between us until he cooled off.

"What're you going to do about it?"

I don't answer because I can't answer and then decide to change the subject. "Do you love me?"

"Of course, I do."

"Is our love strong enough to survive anything."

"Define anything."

"Gill, just..."

He cuts me off before I finish. "How can I know for sure? There are never any guarantees. All we can do is work at it."

"That's not much of an answer."

"We need to talk face to face. When are you coming home? I need you, the office needs you, the First Federal campaign needs you."

"I'm working on that down here and should have it finished by the time I get back."

"And that will be...?"

"Sunday. I want to go to church with Ganzie and I'll leave right after the service."

The phone is like a hot coal in my hand as I dial my home number. I start pressing the numbers, stop, almost drop the receiver, retrieve it, hold it to my ear, start dialing, then stop again. I feel flushed and my stomach is in knots but talking to Roland is something I have to do. The longer I put it off, the worse it will be when I finally see him again.

When I hear his voice yelling on his end of the line, "Where the hell are you?" I almost drop the receiver, actually want to throw it against the wall but compose myself long enough to respond calmly, "Don't shout at me. I'm in Sedalia with Ganzie."

"You just up and disappear without a word and expect me to be calm? I had no idea where you were. I almost called the police but then I called the agency and Erica said you took some vacation. What the hell is going on?"

"Have you forgotten Sunday?"

"So we had an argument, so what?"

"You hit me, Roland. Were you too drunk to remember?"

"Don't start that mess, Neely. Of course, I remember but I didn't mean anything," he says with no sincerity.

"I didn't call to argue. I just wanted you to know where I am. I'll be back on Sunday. Save your yelling for then."

"I'm not yelling," he protests, then adds, "Well, maybe I am yelling, but I'm upset. What do you expect?"

"We can't go on the way we've been and we need to talk about that when I get back."

"Okay, I'll see you when you get home."

"I'll only be there long enough to pick up a few things."

"What the hell are you talking about...?" Roland sputters.

"Later," I say as I slowly drop the receiver from my ear, this time with the certainty of a decision having been made.

Reluctant to be alone at the back of the house, I settle on the couch again, hoping sleep will overtake my thoughts and give my restless mind some peace. However, I toss and turn on the narrow pillows for hours with my eyes closed but my mind on a treadmill reliving my fight with Roland over and over.

30 The Beginning of the End

Last Sunday, I had beat Roland home by only two hours, having spent the previous week with Gill. I raced through the house, unpacking my suitcase and returning it to its proper place in the basement, then picking up the clutter I had left in the wake of my hurried departure.

With time running short, I ran to the kitchen and began pulling things out of the refrigerator and from the cupboards to prepare dinner. By the time I heard his car in the driveway, an out-of-the-jar spaghetti sauce simmered on the stove, pasta boiled in a Dutch oven and a salad was magically appearing in a bowl by the sink. I was exhausted.

'Neely, I'm home,' he called from the living room. Even though every step I danced was to the tune of his imminent arrival, as soon as I heard his voice, I felt instantly intruded upon. Still trying to hold Gill close, I didn't want to lose it all because of Roland's presence.

My ears picked up his every movement. First he stopped at the desk to check the mail. Did I even remember to bring it in? Then he walked the long hallway to our bedroom, his suitcase carelessly bumping against the wall. Then I didn't know where he was and was close to panic when the TV blasted and I knew he was back in the living room. All the while, I maintained my position at the sink tearing lettuce for a would-be salad.

I started to breathe again, imagining him settling into the plush chair to watch a game, and suddenly there he was in the kitchen, walking toward me.

'Great workshop,' he started, leaning to kiss me but the smell of scotch assaulted my nostrils and I moved just enough to cause his face to sideswipe mine.

I tried to concentrate on the tomato I was washing and worked even harder to remember how good Gill made me feel. Roland moved behind me and tried to wrap his arms around me.

'You've been drinking,' I said, twisting my body away from him, moving to the refrigerator for a bottle of salad dressing. There, my mind went blank and Gill's image disappeared.

'What the hell is wrong with you?' he asked, his voice instantly angry. I stiffened and the spike that ran up and down my spine started to hurt. The muscles in my jaw ached with tension.

'Nothing,' I said with pain becoming more and more a reality.

'You act like you don't want me to touch you,' he added sharply.

'I'm trying to fix your dinner.'

Dinner was the least of what I was trying to do and Roland, though unfortunately saturated with alcohol, was still sober enough to figure that out.

He walked to the other side of the room and faced me, like a creature assessing its prey. His eyes narrowed suspiciously. 'What did you do while I was gone?' he asked in a steady voice.

'What do you think I did?'

'I tried to call you,' he tested.

'No, you didn't,' I countered quickly, knowing he was lying.

'I could find out what you did if I really wanted to know.'

'You act like I have something to hide.'

'So tell me what you did and I'll believe you.'

'Tell me what you did. How many bars did you go to? Or is that just an acquired smell since you got back in town?'

'What I did is none of your business.'

With a sharp edge to each word that left my mouth, I said, 'What I did isn't any of your business either.'

'You know, you can be a real bitch...'

'And you are a real bastard.'

Roland crossed the room and struck me on the face all in one motion, his hand raised in the air and his fist connecting with the soft flesh of my cheek before I had time to react.

'That makes things a lot easier,' I said defiantly.

'What things?' He grabbed my shoulders and pulled me close, his eyes glowing with fire.

I tried to extricate myself from his grip but his fingers dug into my shoulders like the tines of a fork. 'You've been drinking, Roland. Let's stop this before it's too late.'

'Fighting with you is a pure pleasure,' he snarled. 'At least, I know you're in the same room with me. Most of the time, I don't know what the fuck you got going on.'

'What's your point?' I asked bitterly.

'This is my point and don't you fucking forget it. If I ever find out you got someone on the side, I'll fucking kill you.' The words flew out of his mouth with venom and the pupils of his eyes were small dark pools of rage. Suddenly he loosened his grip and shoved me away from him so hard I fell against the table and then landed on the floor. The dishes I had placed on the table in preparation for dinner clattered from the sudden jolt. My side felt a sharp jab as it connected with the corner of the table. I moved my hand to cover the wound, but was unable to move or get up.

Roland's hand swung down and when I realized he was not going to help me but rather was preparing to hit me again, I raised my arm and screamed, 'No, please, don't.'

He stopped his fist in mid air, glared at me for a moment then turned and stormed out of the room.

For the first time in all our years together, I was terrified of Roland. What before had been just verbal abuse was now perhaps life-threatening. I didn't know what to do next.

Roland was never moved by tears, so I never cried out loud within his hearing. That night was no exception. The only evidence that I was sobbing was the soft heaving of my defeated shoulders.

31 Things Change

I had fooled myself into thinking I could stay married to a man I didn't love or respect, live my life any way I chose and that none of it mattered. That no decisions had to be made, nothing had to change. But every decision I didn't make just to keep my material world intact created this mess I'm in. How could I have been so careless and why had I failed to notice when things got so bad?

Somehow we've stayed together for fourteen years. Fourteen years of 24-hour days, each hour feeling like an eternity will pass before the next hour begins. Each hour jammed with unnoticed minutes when time quietly chips away all the detail that transpires in a single day.

Between those relentless hours and those fleeting minutes are the spaces where Roland and I have lived, where our movements were recorded and where our existence mattered. It is those spaces that gave our marriage its meaning and it is in those spaces I got lost in the illusion that I could make it work.

In the beginning, there was hope. Then the days bled into each other, each day seeing the end of some things, the beginning of others but all of them merged into insignificant blurs. Nothing stood out, nothing marked a turning point, that irreversible moment when things will never again be what they were before. No particular look, no dead spot in the heart that failed to respond to a kiss, no touch that was more unwelcome than the one before it.

No, nothing remarkable had distinguished one day from the other and yet, subtly, irrevocably, Roland and I had become enemies. Last Sunday should have been like all the other unimportant days, but time imploded and that day moved into the spotlight.

That was the day after which nothing will ever be the same again.

I must have dozed off because when I suddenly am aware that I'm awake, it feels like I've always been awake but I feel disoriented and I don't know where I am. I was in the middle of a dream but I can't recall the details no matter how hard I try to put the pieces of it together. It feels like I was crying in the dream but, awake, I don't know why.

Then it all comes flooding back, my fight with Roland, my escape to Sedalia to seek Ganzie's help and her confession that her beloved husband had fathered a child by another woman. And that child was my mother! And she had raised that child as her own.

Alma, the child of Charleston Sims and Ophelia Lucas!

It is, indeed, the secret of the ages. If Mama knows, she has lived her life with that secret buried deep inside her despicable heart. There's been no hint that she and Ganzie don't share the same blood.

And Joe Spencer!

If Ganzie is trying to help me, it isn't helping. I can't do what she did, stay married to one man while loving another, sacrificing myself for the greater good. If that's her message, I don't want to hear it.

Times have changed. Ganzie didn't believe passion could sustain a relationship; I believe nothing else can. My heart literally floats on the lightness of Gill's voice and the smell of his cologne. If Ganzie felt that way about Joe Spencer, how could she have ever let him go?

My world is upside down and my feet are dangling in the air. I don't know what to feel or what to do; I am lost on a highway that had no origin and has no destination. I feel like I'm about to lose everything.

Near dawn I drift into sleep with fear chilling my blood.

32 Ganzie

The air circulating around the porch is fresh and smells of lily of the valley and iris blooming idly in the soil beyond the steps. It's a good thing they appear year after year without any tending because it's been a long time since I could take care of a garden. Neely and I sit in the old metal chairs that have been on the porch for as long as I can remember and watch the morning skate by. There was a time when my hands would have busied themselves crocheting a doily or stitching an intricate pattern, but now they rest in my lap content with inactivity.

She's leaving after church tomorrow and, for now, I just want to enjoy her presence while I can but melancholy separates us and keeps us from knowing what to say to each other. In the distance only the sound of railroad cars uncoupling break the silence.

Thursday and Friday passed so quickly as Neely helped me sort through old magazines and clothing, things I can't do alone, and we talked about things carrying less weight than our previous conversations. I hope it was a healing time for her so she could make sense of what I told her, accept it and figure out how to move forward.

Now it's Saturday and I am saddened by time running out. I want her to stay longer, afraid I won't ever see her again. I am so weak and tired and know my days are coming to an end.

Neely breaks the silence first. Her voice is somber. "I'm not angry with you; I just don't know what to say."

"I knew it would be hard but you needed to know."

"What did you think I'd do with that information?"

"Everyone needs to know their history. In time, I hope you'll understand that."

"I was better off not knowing."

"You think that now but I'm here to tell you that secrets destroy."

"And the truth will set you free?" she says derisively.

"Look at your mother—she doesn't even know why she's so angry all the time. Nobody escapes their past but knowing it can help you survive it."

Neely gets up and comes to kneel beside my chair and buries her face in my lap. "I need you to be my grandmother." she murmurs.

I stroke her hair and speak in a voice already from the distant future. "I'm still your grandmother. Nothing can change that."

"Do you want me to tell Mama you're ill?" she asks.

"No, but I do want you to talk to her, try to understand her."

"I don't want to go back to Des Moines, Ganzie." She looks up and all I see is Neely, the little girl who wanted to run away from home.

"You have never liked the leaving of any place. But you'll be fine. You'll go home and you'll get things figured out. I have faith in you."

33 The 5th Commandment

Maple Lane is no longer a dirt road on the outskirts of town but rather a paved busy avenue. The old AME Church still stands on its original site, showing its age. My great grandfather's house is long gone but the church remains, a testament to Ganzie's good fight to keep her Papa's dream alive. There is always talk of tearing it down to make way for a shopping mall—the acres of land are too valuable to just sit with memories of the past—but Ganzie's strong will has fought off real estate developers, city planners and merchants. Now, her battle is near its end. It's going to be up to the current congregation to win the war.

I help Ganzie to a pew while the choir, clad in royal blue robes, fill the sanctuary with a moving gospel hymn. Folks sway to an inspirational arrangement of *How Great Thou Art* and all eyes are on the pastor, the Rev. Joseph Shuttleforth, commanding his post behind the pulpit. The service means many things to me beginning and ending with the fact that, in a few hours, I have to leave. Meanwhile, I just want to forget everything except the power of the choir voices and the anticipation of Rev. Shuttleforth's sermon. He is known to preach hellfire and brimstone and today I want a little of each. I tolerate the announcements, the collections and the introduction of visitors waiting for his message.

It's so hot in the un-air-conditioned building that the small paper fan the usher gave me is no match for the humidity that drapes itself over everything. My dress clings to my back and arms and butt while beads of sweat glisten on my skin.

I'm almost ready to leave when Rev. Shuttleforth stands up, assumes a majestic pose and lets his booming voice fill the room.

"My fellow Christians," he starts out low, looking out over the parishioners like the great patriarch he is, "we are here together this morning because we share a common bond. We are the ones," his voice raises a pitch, "who assemble in Gawd's house and worship in His name. We are the ones," he repeats in his deep, resonant voice, "who assemble in Gawd's house and worship in His name. There are those out in the world who are intent on doing worldly things. Did you hear me? I said, there are those out in the world who are intent on doing worldly things. But it is those of us in Gawd's house," he bellows the words now, "who respect and worship...His name.

"One of the Ten Commandments says, 'honor thy father and mother'." His voice softens. "Stop and think about what that means, my fellow Christians. It means, honor the two people who brought you into this world, the two people who deserve your love and respect above all else. But before you can do that, you must take it a step higher." His voices lifts to its highest pitch. "Before you can honor your father and mother, you must honor the Father of all Fathers, the Gawd of all Gawds and His only son, our Lord and Savior, Jesus Christ. That's why we're here this Sunday morning. I said," he shouts with resonance, "there are those out there in the world intent on doing worldly things and then there are those of us in Gawd's house intent on honoring the name of our Father."

His voice becomes quiet again. "Young people today don't recognize the significance of what I'm saying. Young people think what they want to do is all that matters. They forget where they came from and don't know where they're going. Young people need to be reminded of the basic fact that Gawd is the Father and He has made all the rules. Everything they even think of, He has already thought of. I said, everything," his voice bellows again, "they even think of, He has already thought of. To Gawd, there is nothing new, only things not yet done.

"Our fathers and mothers may not be perfect. After all, Gawd is the only perfect being. But our fathers and mothers are Gawd's agents on this earth and they deserve our love and respect..."

I'm riding the cadence of Rev. Shuttleforth's delivery, inspired and full of awe, but the words 'they deserve our love and respect' seem to be directed straight at me and I instantly know that I am searching for the answers to the wrong questions. Instead of worrying about Gill and Roland, I need to first come to terms with the two people who have marked me with their miserable lives, my parents, Alma and Clement Kingston.

Leaving Sedalia is more difficult than I expect. I stuff my suitcase in the front compartment of my VW and turn to see Ganzie struggling down the front steps.

"I would've come back inside to say goodbye," I say.

"The fresh air is good for me," she insists.

I wrap my arms around her and don't want to let go. She breaks the embrace and reaches into her pocket. When her hand comes out, in it is a small gold ring with an opal stone. She presses it into my hand.

"Your grandpa gave me this the Christmas we got engaged. When he told me about Ophelia, I took it off and have never worn it again."

"I can't take it from you."

"I believe he was trying to say he was sorry for something I didn't even know he'd done. Now I want to tell you I'm sorry but you know what I've done and you may never forgive me. I hope the ring will remind you that I love you, have always loved you and never wanted you to be hurt by all that mess."

I take her in my arms again. "I'll call you as soon as I get home."

"Yes, do, but please don't spend your time worrying about me. I'm almost 90 years old. I've lived 90 long, hot summers and enjoyed the golden colors of 90 falls, felt the wrath of 90 winters and seen the pink and white blossoms of 90 springs. In other words, I've seen all the beauty God can bestow on one human being and I couldn't have asked for more. What's more, I'm leaving behind a wonderful granddaughter who will carry on for me."

Tears flow freely down my cheeks and Ganzie reaches up to wipe them away. "I love you, Neely baby," she says, fighting back her own tears, "and don't you ever forget it."

34 Neely

It is a typical Midwest August day with air so torrid it scorches your lungs when you inhale. Even the thistle growing by the roadside is limp from the heat and the few cows visible in the pastures are lying down, too hot and tired to stand while grazing. The sky is cornflower blue with traces of smoky white clouds hovering on the distant horizon though it is difficult to tell whether they are clouds or steam rising from the sweltering pavement.

I left Sedalia about mid afternoon when the heat was at its highest and there's no air-conditioning in my car to protect me from the blistering day. I roll down the window hoping to catch a breeze and a blast of hot air slams into my face. Heading north toward uncertain peril, I am well aware that this is likely my last visit with Ganzie. Feeling an intense desire to stay and yet needing to go, it was difficult to get in the car and drive away. And now, fiercely fighting every mile that takes me away from Sedalia, I can barely breathe. My chest is compressed with the pressure of sweltering heat and anticipated grief.

As the VW sails up Highway 65, the details of Ganzie's life with Charleston Sims and her love for an enigmatic young man named Joe Spencer occupy my thoughts. I thought I knew her so well and it's strange to discover I didn't know her at all. Zelle Simms is more than my 90-year-old grandmother; she is a daughter and a wife but more than that, a woman. A woman with the same hopes and dreams that all women have.

I have never thought of Ganzie as a woman; now I can't think of her any other way.

And there she is, Zelle Marshall, a young woman who let her Papa tell her what to do, let the world tell her what to do.

Zelle Marshall, a young woman so in love with love and so in love with Charleston Sims, a man who wasn't worth the time of day. A weak man, a selfish man, a man who brought shame to her doorstep and expected her to overlook it.

Then a young Zelle Sims, loving a man like Joe Spencer but letting him walk away for good, just watching him walk away...because she thought she shouldn't love him.

And now an old Zelle Sims, who survived a life outside her dreams but found light and joy and wisdom in spite of everything gone wrong, who has the grace to remember love and not regret. Who has the wisdom to forgive if not forget. Who has the compassion to tell the truth in spite of what it might cost.

I cross the Iowa border with a better understanding of what Ganzie wants me to do. She wants me to have the courage to stand on my own two feet, not depend on anybody else and to have the strength to tell the truth no matter what the cost.

I unlock the door to my house with a new sense of purpose. Roland isn't home so it gives me time to pack without his interference. I hurry from room to room, sorting what to take now and what to pick up later. The house is so full of Roland that I can leave most of it behind without missing a thing.

About midnight, I hear the garage door open and know it's time to face the music. I quickly run through the speech I've rehearsed and realize how weak it sounds, but I don't care. Firm in my resolve to leave, I'm prepared to face Roland without fear. I'm closing the lid of the suitcase when he walks into the bedroom and sees all the signs that I'm leaving.

"What are you doing?" he asks as though he can't see half-filled boxes and a closed suitcase on the bed. I don't smell any alcohol and I hope a sober Roland will be easier to manage.

Snapping the suitcase latch, I say simply, "Leaving."

"Leaving?" he asks in a flat voice. "Where are you going?"

"I want a divorce, Roland."

"There's someone else, isn't there?" he asks, glaring at me with that "aha" look, like his suspicions have finally been validated.

I look away. "That's not the point," I answer.

"So there is someone else," he states emphatically.

"Roland, some people grow together in a marriage and they can go on forever. Others grow apart and lose their way.

That's us and I don't think we can find our way again. I don't have the energy to try."

Roland is calmer than I expected. "I know I've been pretty selfish lately," he says.

"Call it what you want, but the truth is you don't give a damn about me."

"There's someone else, isn't there?" he asks again in lower tones, acquiescence clouding his voice.

It's hard to admit, hard to take the blame for, hard to acknowledge that I am about to deal the mortal blow to our fractured marriage. But now is the time for confession, not equivocation.

"Yes," is all I say.

His face simmers with controlled rage as he spits words at me. "If you walk out that door, you leave with nothing—not this house, not a dime from our bank account."

"Half of it is mine," I say defiantly.

"You act like a fucking whore and then think you still deserve half? You better get a lawyer."

"Then keep your shit. Whatever else, I'll leave with a lot more than I came with."

"You bitch...you've lost your fucking mind." With each word his voice moves an octave higher and he hits the word 'mind' with an intensity that frightens me.

"If you hit me, I'll call the police, so help me God."

Roland calms down considerably and says quietly, "I'm not going to hit you. "We can fix this if you…"

I cut him off. "What we had is over. All I'm doing is putting an end to a bad situation."

"How long?"

"How long what?"

"How long have you been seeing this other dude?"

"You don't need to know."

"I need to know for my peace of mind."

"You'll have to look for peace of mind somewhere else."

"I suppose you've got plans with this guy."

"I have no plans."

Then in a low controlled voice simmering with rage, he takes an ugly turn. "Did Ganzie put her stamp of approval on your cheap..."

I cut him off again, my eyes blazing and my words sharp as razor blades. "You know what, Roland? You're a real son of a bitch. This discussion is over."

Then in my grandmother's idiom, I say, "But let me tell you one thing: don't ever mention Ganzie's name in that tone of voice again. If you do, I might kill you."

A deflated Roland says, "I'm sorry, Neely, I didn't mean it. I didn't mean any of it."

"It doesn't matter whether you did or didn't. The fact you said it shows how far we've come down different paths and I'm not traveling on yours anymore."

The Holiday Inn is not exactly where I want to be but it's the best short-term solution I can come up with. By the time I check in, shower and get in bed, I am seething with anger and too tired to sleep. It was more difficult to confront Roland than I thought yet very satisfying. Words I had not even rehearsed came to me at just the moment I needed them and I expressed myself with unusual clarity. I spoke, if not eloquently, at least fearlessly and with certainty. It is a relief to have told Roland exactly what I think of him, our marriage and everything in between. Far too long I've walked on eggshells, afraid to speak my mind and allowing him to crush me with his ego.

Now it's over and the direction I am headed is clear. Mile markers, one after another, stretch out along the path. Roland was the first and I sailed past him without a scratch. Now I'm ready to take on Gill and then, God forbid, my mother. If I can maintain the resolve I had with Roland, I'll be home free and nothing will ever diminish me again.

35 Neely and Gill

The shadowy corners of the hotel room are filled with ghosts as I agonize over what to say to Gill. Sitting on a strange bed with a lumpy mattress smelling of moth balls and disinfectant, I try to forget everything familiar and get used to all things new and frightening. With my knees tucked under my chin and my arms wrapped tightly around my legs, drawing on a newfound and newly tested strength, I plot a plan of action.

Tomorrow I'll go to the office and turn in the First Federal project. Then I'll ask Gill for some time off, go to the bank, draw money out of the savings account before Roland freezes it and go apartment hunting. Then I'll relax for a few days, maybe hire an attorney and then get back to work. A week is all I need, then I can get my life back on track.

The details of the plan seem fairly simple but I quickly waver at the thought of putting them into action.

First of all, Gill won't let me just waltz into his office, turn in the portfolio, ask for time off, then turn around and leave. He'll look at me with questioning eyes; he'll want to know why; he might even get up from his chair, move in my direction and try to take me in his arms (I might be crying). He might even try to kiss me.

And somewhere in the middle of all these things he might do, he'll try to get me to sit down and discuss my plans for us.

Us.

Such a strange concept and I don't even know when we became us.

It began at an office Christmas party. Gill wanted to celebrate a good year so he rented a room, hired a band, a caterer and threw open the bar to his staff and their families. Roland refused to attend and I was pleased to go without him.

Once there, however, I didn't like being alone and made too many trips to the open bar. When the evening was over, my mind was numb, and when Gill sat down at my table, I was in a dark mood.

'Where's Roland?' he asked, flashing a smile.

'Your guess is as good as mine,' I said flatly.

'He shouldn't have let you out of the house by yourself.' He kissed me on the cheek and said gently, 'Don't drink anymore. OK?' Then he walked away.

Next thing I knew, he was back at the table, carrying my coat and singing, 'The Party's Over, it's time to call it a day.' Continuing the melody, he sang, 'You shouldn't drive, why don't you let me take you home?'

'But...' I tried to say but Gill was already shoving my arms into the sleeves of my coat.

In the parking lot I threw up. My head was swimming, my stomach was queasy and before I could stop it, a wave of nausea surged upward. Quickly I turned away from Gill so he couldn't see everything I had eaten during the evening splash on the pavement. Embarrassed and humiliated, I collapsed into his car.

'Are you okay?' he asked with concern.

'Throwing up always helps a drunk.'

'Don't be so hard on yourself.'

I looked at him with the large, soulful eyes of a wounded puppy. Any second, I thought I was going to throw up again but I closed my eyes, took a few deep breaths and waited for the feeling to subside.

'You need some hot, black coffee,' Gill offered. 'How about it?'

'I'm not sure it'll help,' I balked.

'It might. If nothing else, it'll give you time to feel better before you go home.'

He was right, I didn't want to walk in the house with alcohol on my breath, the way Roland did more and more. So I nodded my head in agreement, not realizing we were about to embark on something that would make me never want to go home again.

'How did this happen?' I asked in dismay, furious with myself for making love to a man who was too much like Roland to be worth it. I barely remembered the transition from the coffee shop to his bed. I don't think he asked because I surely would have said no. But somewhere in the middle of a hug to console my tears and a kiss that started on my cheek and ended on my lips, there was a surge of feelings we didn't even know were there. At least, I didn't.

Gill said smugly, 'This was going to happen eventually. I knew it the first day I saw you.'

'That's a rotten thing to say,' I said hotly.

'It's not rotten. I've always felt something was going to happen between us. Like it was our karma or something.'

'Well, this shouldn't have happened. You're my boss and I'm married.'

'If Roland treated you right, you wouldn't be here.'

'How he treats me is none of your business. As for you, if I closed my eyes, you could be him.'

'How can you say that? What's wrong with me?'

'You're arrogant and you don't believe in anything,' I said bluntly.

'I believe in lots of things, but they all begin and end with enjoying life,' he answered with a twisted smile that made me angry.

'There's nothing noble about that,' I countered.

'I'm not aiming for nobility.'

'Maybe you should.'

'Look, I learned a long time ago that you can't please everybody. I know who I am and what I want out of life and the rest of the world can go to hell.'

'What makes you so hostile?'

'I am not hostile and you know it. Inside here beats a heart of gold.' He palmed the left side of his chest and tapped it lightly with his fingers.

'Then why do you keep it such a big secret from everyone else?'

'Not secret, Babe, just sacred.'

'You know you can be a real jerk, don't you?'

'A jerk? Maybe, but I don't hurt anybody so what does it matter?'

'If we mix this...,' I started, then hesitated. I looked at Gill with question marks in my eyes, trying to see something in his face I recognized. Then I finished my sentence. 'I could get hurt, personally and professionally.'

'People hurt themselves, Neely. I will never hurt you and I will never let anything else hurt you.'

'You can't guarantee that.'

'I will never hurt you,' he repeated emphatically. 'You just make sure you don't let yourself get hurt.' He punctuated the word 'get' with another tap to his heart.

'I take it back, you're not a jerk, you're an asshole.'

He threw up his hands in protest, laughed suggestively, and said, 'I really don't think you should call your boss an asshole.' Then he pulled me close and kissed me.

'We can't do this, Gill,' I protested.

'We are doing this,' he replied, kissing me deeply and running his hands the length of my body.

'We're making a big mistake.'

'If we don't, you're fired...'

The words got lost as we began to make love again. I yielded completely to the sensation of Gill moving inside my body. It was an all-consuming pleasure I would seek to recreate over and over again.

A few days later he looked up from his desk when I entered his office. We had barely spoken since the night of the party and the tension was palpable. I was slipping away from him, lost inside my regret about our lovemaking, and he knew it.

'Can you get away long enough to have a drink after work?'

'It's not a good idea.'

'It's the only idea I have.'

'Gill...'

'Neely...don't stop us before we even get started.'

I met him at Dinado's, a hangout for our informal staff meetings, and my intention was to do exactly that—stop before it was too late. I couldn't imagine entering into a relationship with my boss or getting close enough to him to get hurt. But as I looked into his eyes, the pizza getting cold and the beer growing warm, I could only think of his kisses on my shoulders.

He, too, seemed preoccupied with some distant memory, trying hard to bring it back into focus. Finally, he took my hands into his and whispered huskily, 'We can't solve this here. Let's go home,' as if his apartment was already ours and it were only natural that we would retreat to the comfort of our own private domicile.

Later, in Gill's arms, a sober me allowed myself to relax, to enjoy his caresses and to yield to the pleasure of his lovemaking. I felt deliciously wild and free and was able to shut out the entire world so that nothing could infringe on our pleasure. I surrendered any lingering misgivings to the crush of his body and allowed the force of his embrace to remind me that nothing else mattered.

'We're good together,' he said when we were resting quietly. 'I see a great future for us.'

'But Roland...'

Gill narrowed his eyes and let the corners of his mouth curve in a barely discernable smile. 'Let's just have a good time,' he said quietly, 'and pretend you don't belong to him.'

36 Living A Lie

In the beginning our relationship didn't seem all that important. We didn't have the luxury of being alone together whenever we wanted but we saw each other in the office every day and our private intimacy made our business relationship electric. There were looks and touches that I feared didn't go unnoticed by the staff and Gill began talking to me more and more about the business end of the agency. He mentored me on several important projects and the palm of his hand on my back while we were talking would almost make me forget what he was saying.

We fell into a pattern of working all day, stopping at Dinado's after work for a drink and, when we could, spending a few hours alone in his apartment. My standard excuse to Roland was that I was "working late" but when I got home, he was usually in bed or not even at home so I fooled myself into believing that I was getting away with it.

My days split into segments that couldn't touch each other: my work life and all the hours I spent with Gill and my life with Roland. I was so driven by my feelings that I didn't think much about what would happen if Roland found out. It was exciting to be in the clutches of new romance but I always thought I could take it or leave it. I didn't plan to leave Roland nor did I see Gill in my world permanently.

But slowly, quietly, without any warning, what began as a simple attraction evolved into something deeper and more meaningful than mere chemistry. I was afraid to call it love but found myself wanting to be with Gill and putting more energy and thought into making that happen.

Eventually I learned that Gill was not like Roland at all. His outward display of arrogance was merely a shield to protect his vulnerable side.

'I don't want that responsibility,' he said when I told him how much his staff admired him.

'What responsibility, Gill?'

In a measured tone, he said, 'The responsibility of their admiration.'

'I don't understand,' I said, clearly confused by his adamant response.

He was blunt with his explanation.

'If I accept their admiration, eventually I'll let them down and they'll blame me for everything that's wrong with their lives. I don't want to be in that position. I'd rather they just work hard and do a good job.'

That was the heart of what Gill was and what he was not. Never wanting to let anybody down and never wanting to be blamed for anything. I understood it completely. I had spent most of my life avoiding the same responsibility.

'You can't stop people from admiring you, you know.'

'No, but I sure can discourage it.'

'Is that why you don't let people get close to you,' I asked, hoping he would open up and let me into his world; that he knew how much I loved him.

'You're close to me,' he responded, pulling my body into his.

'I don't mean physically, you idiot. I mean, emotionally.'

'You're close to me,' he repeated with the narrow slant of his eyes that I could never read.

Then two weeks ago Roland went to a conference giving us nearly a week alone so we took advantage of the freedom and drove to Minnesota. It was our first trip together, the first time we could go where we wanted and not care if anybody knew us and the first time waking up with each other the next morning. I enjoyed every minute of it until it was time to leave. My two worlds caved in on each other and I didn't want to go back to the one Roland lived in.

Gill didn't understand my distress and it made me angry. 'You act like we have all the time in the world,' I fired at him hotly.

'Relax. We've got lots of time.'

'We've got no time. Tomorrow we have to go back and...' The rest of the unfinished sentence was, '...we'll be living our secret lie again.' I couldn't say it because I didn't want to live it. It was too much to bear.

'What's wrong, Babe?' he asked. 'I've never seen you like this.'

'I think we need to talk.' There, at last I said the words that could ease my pain...or make it worse.

'About what?' he asked apprehensively.

Even with the stage set, the words were hard to form. I started, stopped, and then started again. Finally they all came out at once. ‘I can’t pretend with Roland anymore. I’m afraid he’ll be able to sense you merely by looking at me. I can’t go on this way.’ Then my eyes caught his and held them fast. ‘We can’t go on this way.’

‘Leave him,’ Gill stated, confident that he offered the obvious solution to my predicament. His eyes narrowed to stress his point.

We had never discussed a future together and now, with this quiet assertion, it was out in the open. But I was unprepared to think about what leaving Roland meant so I continued talking as though I hadn't heard him.

‘In the beginning, it was simpler, so much easier to manage. What we were doing didn’t bother me very much. I guess I thought it would always be that way.’

‘Leave him,’ Gill repeated, each word underscored with lines of certainty.

‘Yes, I could leave him,’ I acknowledged but then added a certainty of my own, ‘or you and I could end it.’

‘We can't end it and you know it.’

‘We can,’ I stated emphatically, ‘and maybe that's exactly what we should do.’

Gill's deep, melodic voice took on a somber tone. ‘What would happen to us if we did? I had nothing, zero, nada before we got together. What did you have?’

‘We don't have anything now.’

‘We have a lot. Leave him and we can have everything.’

‘What is everything, Gill?’

'It's what exists on this side of infinity. It's how I feel when I think of you, when I see you, when we're together and when we make love. It's how I hope I make you feel.'

His words were beautiful, even poetic, more than I could have hoped for in my wildest fantasy, but still a trail of doubt followed them into my ears.

'We hardly know each other,' I replied, more to the misgivings crawling up and down my arms than to him.

'Our reality is measured by more than just minutes and hours. You can't quantify it, so don't try.'

'Sometimes I don't know what's real and what isn't.'

'Neely, I love you. That's real.'

The word *love* shocked me. I never expected him to say it and I doubt he ever planned to let it escape his lips.

'But more than love you, I *am* you,' he added. 'In addition to being me, I'm everything that's you. Because of you I am more complete, less defensive, less angry, less sarcastic, more settled with myself. I'm 38 goddamned years old; I've been married, divorced and dragged through the mud. But I've never had a relationship that made me feel this way. You think I want to give it up?'

I was touched. Gill had dipped into the pit of my worst fears and was trying to pull me to safety. It made me love him all the more but my feet were not yet on firm ground.

'Why me?' I asked, not expecting to believe his answer.

'I don't know why you. I don't even know when you. It just is you. Isn't that enough?'

'Most of the time it is, but sometimes...'

'You've let Roland destroy your spirit. I can't help you get it back unless you want it back.'

'I'm not sure I ever had it in the first place.'

'Look, you're a grown woman, Neely. You don't have to live with those ghosts anymore. You can decide who you are and how you want to live your life. You're in charge.'

'And you're a sarcastic SOB,' I said, needing to deflect the intensity of our exchange.

'Well, you wouldn't want me to lose my essence, would you?'

'No, not your essence, just your veneer.'

'There's nothing wrong with my veneer.' He then tapped his chest and rubbed his skin.

'No, it's a good veneer,' I said, moving his fingers to kiss the spot he had just tapped. 'I didn't plan it to be this way, you know,' I added, the words smothered by the proximity of my lips to his skin.

'Neely, look at me,' he said, cupping the side of my face and making me look at him. 'I didn't plan any of this either. I didn't look for it or even want it, but it's here and now I don't want to lose it.'

'Neither do I.'

'Then what's all this about?'

'We've never made a plan for anything, let alone the future. We just act out our feelings and let the chips fall where they may.'

'Leave him,' Gill said one more time.

'That's just my point. I never knew you wanted me to.'

'Well, I was afraid to push you too far. I thought those chips would fall in place in time.'

'And how much time did you think it would take?'

'What do you want me to say?'

'I don't want to put words in your mouth.'

'Look,' he said, kissing me gently. 'This is our last night in paradise. Let's make believe it's never going to end. When we get back to Des Moines, we'll work out the serious stuff.'

'You're right. Tonight is not the time and this is not the place.' Our lips met again and the lightness of the touch was like a sensuous caress. A chill shivered up and down my arms, expanded my rib cage and moved across my abdomen.

'No, this is the place,' he whispered, pretending to bite my neck. 'Or maybe this is the place,' his fingers touched my breasts. 'Or maybe here...'

Our lips became enmeshed in a kiss that was the focus of everything good between us. We drifted into a lovemaking that was passionate yet more relaxed than before, the kind that would consume the hours of the night with its slow intensity.

37 Decisions and Revisions

Now on the hotel bed, I tighten my arms around my legs like a vise and hold myself together with sheer will. What do I tell Gill about us? I don't know where to start, where to finish and what to say in between.

First, I have to tell him that I've left Roland but he'll never understand that my reasons are not his, but my own. 'Leave him,' he said in Minnesota and he'll believe I'm acting on his directive.

He'll want to know *what next* and that I don't know. I don't have the slightest idea if we can make it as a couple and I should tell him so. But he won't accept my answer. Nor will he understand.

The room swirls with images of Gill, my boss and Gill, my lover. I've been stupid to mix business with pleasure and now both are lost.

I don't know if I can do this by myself. Without Ganzie helping me think it through and making sure I'm doing everything the right way, I don't even know where to start. But she expects me to figure this one out on my own. What's more, she's not going to be around to hold my hand anymore.

At that moment, the reality of Ganzie dying hits me square between the eyes and I feel real pain. What am I going to do without the person who has held my life together all these years? No one else understands me, accepts me for what I am and only wants the best for me. Ganzie is everything past, present and future and my life is over without her in it.

I slip into a deep blue funk, asking questions that have no answers and feeling emotions I have no words to describe.

Who I am, why is my life such a mess and why does any of it matter?

I picture a tall, handsome Charleston Sims making love to Ophelia Lucas yet proposing to a hapless Zelle. Then I imagine Alma as a little girl, loving her Papa with all her heart but not understanding the cold woman who took her mother's place.

Then I think of Ganzie and Joe Spencer and wonder what would have happened if they had stayed together. One step down the path with Joe Spencer would have changed my life in ways I can't even comprehend. Maybe I wouldn't have been born because Alma's life would have been different, too. Maybe she would never have married Clement Kingston and I would not exist.

In these reflections, I find only empty spaces and hollow images, nothing tangible to hold on to, nothing to give me answers to the questions of my life or even point me in the right direction. The past is blocked by years of secrecy and will never fully be revealed.

If Ganzie thinks I'll find my future by knowing the past, she is wrong.

I am looking for more than peace of mind; I am looking for peace of heart. Ganzie found it and managed to live her life with a serenity to be envied by anyone still looking. But my heart is full of chaos and I don't understand anything anymore.

I feel like screaming out loud. All my thoughts jumble together and nothing makes any sense. Talking to Gill is the only way to bring things into perspective. Yes, I need to talk to Gill as soon as possible.

On Monday morning, I call him, no longer sure that talking will help.

"I'm glad you're back," he says. "I was really worried about you."

"I apologize for cutting out the way I did. I was very upset."

"You had every reason to be. I just wish you'd called me. I would've slugged the bastard."

"We need to talk. Are you free for dinner?"

"Can you get away?"

"I can get away from now until forever."

"What's going on?" he asks, his voice expressing bewilderment.

"Meet me at Dinado's after work," is all I say.

When I arrive at Dinado's, Gill is already there. On the table is a pitcher of beer and a large pizza. As I approach the booth, he looks up and smiles but his smile fades when he sees the bruise on my cheek which is now several shades of blue and yellow. I sit down and he pours me a beer and shoves the mug toward me. He reaches out and touches my cheek and I push his hand away.

"Does it hurt?" he asks.

"Not anymore," I reply simply.

"I want to kill the bastard," he says vehemently.

Ignoring this, I say, "I've left him."

Gill exhales a sigh of relief. "It's about time," he responds happily.

"I knew you'd feel that way."

"Damn straight. Now we can get on with *our* life."

I cut him off. "Hold it. I can't go from one relationship to another without some space in between."

"But I thought you loved me."

"That's not the point.

"What am I missing here? I thought once you made up your mind about Roland, then you and I would have a chance."

"We do have a chance, but I need some time to sort things out."

"What things?"

"I've got to figure out who I am."

"You know who you are."

"I thought I did but now I'm not so sure."

"What's wrong, Babe?"

"Ganzie told me she's not my mother's natural mother and I don't know anything anymore."

He looks shocked but says simply, "What does it have to do with us?"

"It has everything to do with us."

"Not unless you want it to."

"It doesn't matter what I want. I don't know who I am or what I should do."

"You're the same person you were before you found out."

"Well, I didn't know who that person was either," I snap.

"Look, you don't have to figure this out by yourself, Neely. I can help you."

"No one can help me. I have to do it alone."

Gill takes my hands in his and says quietly, "So is the end for us?"

"I don't know, I don't know. I need some time to sort things out."

"Do you love me?"

"I'm not sure of anything at this point."

"Well, if you don't, it's better to tell me now and get it over with. I don't want to be hurt any more than you do."

"You won't be hurt."

"You don't know what I'll be..." His voice is edgy and his eyes glower with a simmering anger.

I stop him before he says something we'll both regret. "Gill, I just need some time."

His voice softens. "If we're meant to be together, we will be. It's just that simple."

"Thanks," is all I say.

"So, what's the next step? We stop seeing each other for awhile, I mean, just until you get things figured out?"

"I don't want to make any plans for our future. I need to get through the divorce and see what's left of me after."

"What about work?"

"I'll still work if that's okay with you. I need to keep busy."

"Then it's settled. Take all the time you need."

38 Neely

Gill down, Alma Kingston next. I want to delay the confrontation as long as possible because I don't have the slightest idea what to say to her. Mama and I don't communicate well so I know the timing has to be perfect and the words need to be precise. But Ganzie asked me to talk to her so I'll try.

In my hotel room, many false starts are rehearsed and discarded and no complete sentences are formed.

"Ganzie told me she's not..." No, that's too abrupt.

"Tell me about your real..." No, that's actually cruel.

"Why didn't you ever tell me..." No, that assumes a secret knowledge perhaps not true.

In the end I decide to just call her and tell her where I am. But when she answers the phone, even that is hard.

"I've left Roland and I'm staying at the Holiday Inn."

There's silence on her end of the line.

"Did you hear me, Mama?" I ask with great irritation.

"Yes, I heard you, Neely."

"Well, say something."

"What do you want me to say?" After years of saying whatever she pleased, the crisp edge to her words carries a false, hostile note. "If you think leaving Roland is the right thing to do, why do you care what I think?"

"I just hoped I could talk to you about it."

"You've already made up your mind. What can I possibly add?"

There are no nice words to answer such an aggressive question and I have no energy to fight so it's my turn to be silent. Years of bitterness layered with chilly resentment coat the telephone line and there's no way to get back to warmth.

For as far back as I can remember, there has never been a time when soft, non-barbed words left my mother's lips. Her requests were always commands, her questions, condemnations and her answers, caustic lye.

I want to scream, 'I just need someone to talk to,' but I do not. Instead I say icily, "Good night, then, Mother."

I hang up the phone with my heart low to the ground. Talking to Alma will never work. Hell will have frozen over for 1000 years before I'll be able to tell her Ganzie's story. But my grandmother wants me to do it and I want to please her so I'll have to try again. I don't know the time or the place or how I'll get out the first word but I'll definitely try again, just not now.

39 Ganzie's Legacy

I didn't know when I left Sedalia on Sunday it was the last time I would see Ganzie alive. Hope is such a seductive force it carries you beyond the end in sight to a next time that's impossible. In spite of how ill Ganzie is, I've been hoping beyond hope that she'll see her 89th birthday in October, only two months away. That isn't asking too much. But when the call comes from Mr. Dixon on Wednesday, I know it is.

"Mr. Dixon, what's wrong?" I ask fearfully when I answer my office phone. How did he even know this number? There is only one person who could give it to him. That's a good sign. That means Ganzie is well enough to tell him.

But it doesn't get any better than that.

"Your gran'ma aksed me to call you so's she could talk to you."

I stop breathing when I hear Ganzie's voice. "Hello, sweetheart...," she says barely above a whisper.

"How are you feeling?" I ask anxiously, beginning our final conversation by asking such a trivial question.

"Not as good as when you were here," she responds between labored gasps, the words struggling out of her lungs one by one.

"Are you in any pain?" The thought of her suffering causes me to grimace.

"No, no pain, just very tired..." she says, gasping for every word.

"Then don't talk, just listen. I'll be down tomorrow. I'll bring you back to Des Moines and put you in the hospital here. When you get better, you can live with me."

I talk fast to outrun the shadows moving slowly and steadily toward Ganzie's spirit.

"Neely, don't, you mustn't..." but she can't finish her sentence.

Fear overwhelms the strength I try to hold inside my heart and tears rolls down my face. "I'll be there tomorrow as soon as I can get there. Maybe I can make it before noon... just rest comfortably and I'll see you soon."

"Neely, you must listen," she persists.

"Don't talk, Ganzie, please don't talk."

"I have to tell you something..."

"You can tell me tomorrow."

"I must tell you now." Ganzie pauses. "You probably think I don't approve of your Gill..."

"Please don't try to talk," I beg again.

But Ganzie persists, "If I had it to do over again, I would have chosen love."

Her words have a finality impossible to ignore and I say simply, "I'll see you tomorrow."

Hold on, please, hold on until I get there.

The night, however, is far too long and Ganzie can't wait for morning. The phone call comes before I have the chance to travel the miles to Sedalia one more time. I am turning over on the lumpy mattress for perhaps the tenth time and punching the flat pillows, looking for a cool spot on which to rest my cheek when the phone on the nightstand rings.

It's Mama.

"Ganzie died about a half hour ago. The hospital just called. I didn't even know she was sick. Did you know she was sick? Lord knows, she kept everything such a secret from me."

"Mama, will you just shut up," I shout, with anger replacing the surprise of death.

"Don't be so hateful," she pleads with unusual tones of conciliation in her voice. "Ganzie just died! You act like you're the only one who cared about her. She was my mother, after all."

I recoil at her words but realize this is definitely not the time or place to respond. Ganzie must be at my shoulders, holding me tight, making it easier to not lash out and say things I'll regret forever.

Mama hastily fills the void. "Anyway, I'll call Mr. Dixon to get things started so we don't have to rush down. We'll have some things to attend to, but Ganzie didn't have much. I don't think it will take long."

Ganzie relaxes her grip; maybe even pushes me into the next words because when I speak, I literally explode. "You act like we can waltz down there, board up the house and come back home without a thought to what Ganzie would have wanted."

"I'm not going to fight with you at this of all times. Of course, we'll take care of what's necessary, but I still don't think it will take long."

"It will take as long as it takes and I'm not going to rush it. I'm going down today. If you don't want to come with me, you can come later. I really don't care."

"Of course, I'll go with you. How else would I get there?"

I cut her words off quickly, not wanting to hear this placating tone in her voice. I have things to discuss with her and need to remain distant to make it possible. "You can come with Daddy," I say sharply.

Mama confirms what I know to be true. "I don't think he'll go," she says. "He's not one to handle funerals."

It's only one on the list of the many things he can't handle, but I don't care anymore. He's an apathetic old man who has never had two kind words for me and I'm glad he won't be part of Ganzie's farewell.

"I'll call you when I'm on my way to pick you up," I say, then hang up the phone without saying goodbye.

Alone with my grief, I try to comfort myself with memories of Ganzie, but it's impossible. The woman I thought I knew has become a stranger, someone whose public face was a far cry from her private heart, someone who perhaps didn't love me after all. I don't want to think like that, but my jumbled emotions keep getting it all confused. I don't know who Ganzie was, who I am or what's next.

Soon I have to talk to Mama about Ophelia Lucas. To keep it to myself will only perpetuate the lie. But where to begin to tell a story that will change our lives forever? And my mother won't be the most receptive audience. I've never been able to talk to her about anything, great or small.

When I was growing up, if I expressed my thoughts out loud, they were met with harsh criticism, as if I didn't have a brain in my head. If I needed something, I had to justify its necessity. If I just wanted something frivolous, it was normally denied.

Or given at a great price.

Like the time I asked for a new dress to wear to a dance. Roland was my date and I wanted to look special. Definitely a want, not a need.

'Mama,' I began cautiously. 'Next month we're having a dance here on campus and I've been asked to go.'

She could see the dark side to any silver lining and her reply was what I had come to expect.

'I hope you've been attending to your school work, Neely, and not worrying about some boy.'

It was not going to be easy at all.

But it was more than a bottle of cologne or a pair of shoes; it was a dress to wear on a date with Roland Watts. It needed to be perfect and I wanted it very badly. So I persisted.

'No, Mama, I'm not worrying about some boy. But this is the Spring Formal and everyone is going.'

'Is it sponsored by the school?'

'Yes, Mama, it's not a wild party. It's a school dance.'

'Who's this boy and why did he ask you?'

It was the same question I'd asked myself every day since he called but Mama gave it a validity I couldn't ignore.

'Neely, are you crying?' Mama asked sharply, angry at my apparent distress.

I pulled myself together enough to talk.

'No, Mama,' I said.

'What is it you want this time?'

'I don't have a dress to wear.'

'What about the dress I made for your senior prom? It would look awfully pretty and you never did wear it.'

I had actually feigned sickness not to wear that dress. Now I was braver.

'It's not the sort of thing everyone wears here.'

'I don't know, Neely, your father just made a tuition payment. You know how he'll feel about a dress you really don't need.'

'Please, Mama, I won't ask for anything else this year,' I begged. 'And I'll work this summer to pay you back.'

'I'll ask your father but I wouldn't count on it if I were you.'

Not much was worth the kind of raw, salt-in-the-wound, stinging humiliation smoldering inside me.

In the end, neither was Roland Watts.

Yes, I'll have a hard time talking to Alma Kingston. I'll have to stretch all the way to the bottom of my soul to find the place that will give me the courage to do it. I don't know when the right moment will present itself, but when the time comes, I know what I'll say. For now I curl into a ball and try to ease the pain of loss.

40 Requiem for Ganzie

With Mama at my side, I cover the distance between Des Moines and Sedalia in painful silence. The absence of Ganzie is already pressing the air out of my lungs and my chest hurts every time I take a breath. Fully aware I can't keep my grandmother on this earth, my heart refuses to let her go. All I want is a little more time with her, to talk to her, to understand the meaning of all the things she told me. Yet every mile brings me closer and closer to the reality that I will soon have to say good-bye.

It is our last visit I want embedded in my memory, not the body in the satin-lined casket with its cold, waxy, face and immobile features. And then to see that casket lowered into the ground, knowing Ganzie is inside, is more than I can bear.

Ganzie would understand my absence if I stayed away; she would forgive my inability to cope. But I need to stop the pain, to breathe again and there was only one way to say a proper farewell: to attend the public ritual, to see the body in its deathly pallor and to say goodbye out loud.

And, if I am ever to meet my mother on the same plateau, it will begin at Ganzie's funeral.

The miles between Des Moines and Sedalia might be a perfect time for mother and daughter to talk but I'm not ready. Every time I try to form phrases in my mind, I realize I might never be ready. Yet I know it's what Ganzie wants.

In one flash, I fear my grandmother let go of life to force me to talk to Mama. Did she think she had to leave this earth to make it happen? That thought takes me from tears to anger and back to tears again. I don't need a mother as much as I need my grandmother. Eventually, Mama would have learned the truth. It doesn't really matter when.

Ganzie didn't need to die for that.

I only occasionally acknowledge there is someone else in the car. Questions like, 'Do you need to go to the bathroom?' or 'Are you hungry?' are the only words I extend to my mother and she says 'yes' or 'no' and that's it.

By the time we pull into Ganzie's driveway, the tension between us couldn't be cut with a machete. I lug the suitcases from the car and step onto the porch ignoring my mother who follows a few seconds behind. Mrs. Dixon greets us at the door.

"I'm so sorry, Alma," she says, extending her arms for a hug.

"Thank you, Mizz Dixon," Mama answers, accepting the embrace of Ganzie's neighbor and friend.

Mrs. Dixon prattles on in the same dialect her husband speaks. "Neely, I know'd your heart is broken. But I'm here to tell you, your grandmaw was happy as a lark when you was down here last week. She talked about nothin' but you even when she could hardly talk."

Mama shoots daggers at me. "You were down here last week?" she asks in surprise. Her question is a demand to know.

I accept Mrs. Dixon's warm embrace and look sharply at my mother but don't respond.

"Mister Dixon's over to the church but he'll be back soon and then we can get over to the funeral home. I know'd y'all must be hungry, just gettin' off the road and all. What can I get for you?"

It irritates me that she speaks so nonchalantly about the funeral home, about food and about just getting off the road, but then I realize I'm not being fair. After all, it's Mrs. Dixon who's been with Ganzie day after day, feeding her, taking care of her house and being with her up to the very end. And Mrs. Dixon probably understands death a whole lot more than I do and has a faith in the hand of God I myself do not have. I need something exactly like that and am desperate in its absence.

The next two days go by in a blur as I let Mama take over and finalize the funeral arrangements. I feel I have nothing to contribute as she contacts relatives in Columbia and as far away as St. Louis and Kansas City. I also defer to her judgment when it's time to select the casket, the hymns for the service and the text for the funeral program. It isn't until I'm actually in the church and Reverend Shuttleforth takes the pulpit to give the eulogy that I come to life again.

The night before I was numb, even developed a slight fever and then went to bed with dry eyes. However, when Reverend Shuttleforth starts to speak, I am painfully aware of what is happening and tears again choke at the back of my throat and spill from my eyes.

Reverend Shuttleforth delivers an inspired sermon, one Ganzie would have liked. He eulogizes her without over-sentimentality and he speaks in words that mean something to those who knew her well.

"Gawd has taken Clozelle Sims home," he opens in his well-known preacher drawl. "Yes, I said Gawd," he raises his voice an octave, "has taken Clozelle Sims home because I know deep in my heart that's where she has gone. Home to be with Gawd. Home," his voice is almost singing now, "where there is no more pain and suffering. That's what I said. No more pain and suffering. Because if you all don't know it, Clozelle Sims was suffering on this earth. She kept mighty quiet about it, but she suffered nonetheless and now Gawd has said, no more suffering."

Mama glares at me again. She's obviously furious that I was in Sedalia last week and didn't tell her that Ganzie was sick. But Ganzie asked me not to plus I had no way of knowing there was so little time. She touches my arm and I return her glare. Only Reverend Shuttleforth's deep, booming voice breaks the unforgiving visual exchange between us.

"Gawd," he bellows, "has intervened and said, no more suffering. And He has taken His faithful servant home to be with Him. We here on earth will miss her and weep for her loss, but we always knew she was going home to Gawd. We knew that, didn't we?" He almost laughs in the middle of his thought. "Of course, we did. So what better time than now when life had begun to fail her? I say, what better time than *now*," he roars, "when life had begun to fail her.

"She was a good Christian woman, Clozelle Sims was, daughter of Clozer and Sarah Marshall, wife of Charleston Sims and mother of Alma, grandmother of Neely, sister to Ivy and Jeremiah and friend, relative and teacher to many. Everyone loved Clozelle Sims because she gave love to everyone who knew her. She dedicated her life to her family, her community, to her church but, most of all, she dedicated her life to Gawd.

"Folks who knew her and loved her will not forget her and now Gawd will take her into His kingdom and keep her safe with Him for eternity. We can all learn something from the life she lived." His voice gradually lowers in octaves and when he gets to the end, he says quietly, "Now let us pray."

My attention strayed when Reverend Shuttleforth said 'mother of Alma' and I barely hear the prayer that rumbles behind my thoughts. "Heavenly Father," the preacher says reverently, "take Clozelle Sims into Your heart and keep her safe. She was a good woman and she will serve You well in heaven. Help those of us left behind to accept our loss and help us know that she is in a better place. Please Gawd," he raises both arms high, "we beseech You to ease our pain just as You have eased her pain.

"Someday our time will come and we want to be welcome in Your home just as she is. Thank You, Gawd, for the time You let us have her with us. Thank You for all that You have done for us and will continue to do. Thank You in the name of Your son, Jesus Christ. Amen."

I sit in stunned silence. Sadness envelops me like a heavy winter coat worn on the hottest day of summer. I am suffocating from its confinement. I then say my own prayer to alleviate my anguish. "Dear God, keep my Ganzie safe and keep her close. And please, God, give me the strength and wisdom to do the right thing."

At the gravesite, I am numb with grief while Mama stands impassively at my side. Even when I step up to the casket to place a rose for Ganzie to take to heaven with her, Mama says nothing. Mr. Dixon steps between us and tries to bridge the gap.

"Alma, Neely," he says gently, "me and the missus want you to know how sorry we are for your loss." He takes me in one arm and Mama in the other and gives an encouraging squeeze. Then he walks away leaving us struggling with our inability to comfort each other.

41 A Time to Kill

Back at the house, relatives, neighbors and friends of Ganzie, people I don't know are filling up the rooms of Ganzie's house, eating and visiting and exchanging anecdotes about the woman everyone adored. This leaves me alone, preoccupied with thoughts of talking to Mama. Now that Ganzie is gone, the words are forming on my tongue and have to be spoken before I lose my nerve. I watch Mama mingling with the guests, chatting with relatives she hasn't seen in years and I wait.

Late that evening after everyone has gone, I find her in the kitchen washing dishes, cleaning up after the long, chaotic day and the time seems right. If not right, then necessary. I can't stand the strain of silence any longer.

"Mama, I have to talk to you," I begin.

"This really isn't the time." She continues dipping her hands in warm, sudsy water and does not look at me.

"Trust me, there will never be a better time."

"If you insist, but let me warn you, I'm in no mood for any nonsense about you and Roland. You two should patch things up. There's nothing he could have done that would be worth ending your marriage."

"There you go, off on your own tangent without even knowing what I have to say," I snap, both angry and sad that I let her get under my skin so easily.

"Well, what do you have to say?" she asks with bitterness lacing her words.

The anger prevails over the sadness and spurs me on. I am going to reveal the secret about Ophelia Lucas no matter how much it may hurt Mama to break open that long hidden wound.

"Tell me about your mother," I blurt out. It's not what I plan to say but it's what comes out, dredged from my soul by a force I can no longer suppress.

"What do you mean? You knew Ganzie better than anyone."

"I mean, your real mother."

There is a long pause as Mama lifts her hands out of the dishwater and dries them on a nearby towel. Shades of melancholy pass across her face. Then her eyes flicker gravely at me for a fraction of a second, then focus on some distant place.

"Ganzie just died, Neely," she says sharply. "How can you bring up such a subject?"

I am being pushed by a compelling need to tell the truth, maybe more to the point, to test the truth. I feel Ganzie's presence, standing behind me, holding me closely, whispering into my ear, urging me onward.

"When I visited Ganzie last week, she told me that she wasn't your real mother."

I watch my words hit their target like arrows on a mission. A look of distant recollection crosses Mama's face and then her eyes turn dark. "Why were you down here last week anyway? And why were you keeping it from me?"

"That's none of your business. I just want to know about Grandpa Charles and Ophelia Lucas."

"And that's none of your business."

"Ganzie made it my business," I say hotly.

"She was getting a bit senile, I suspect," Mama says easily, thinking she has nothing to fear.

"There was nothing senile about the woman I talked to."

Mama sits down in the wooden kitchen chair and leans back to support her thoughts. She is silent for a long time while I stand, determined to forge ahead. Finally, she speaks, her voice soft and no longer contentious.

"You knew Ganzie was dying and you didn't say a word."

"She asked me not to."

"What did she tell you about Ophelia Lucas?"

I am startled that, with so little effort, the first layer is revealed. I didn't expect it to be so easy. "Then you remember..."

"Of course, I remember. Not very much, but I remember."

"Why have you never told me?"

"It wasn't something we ever talked about."

"That's what Ganzie said...," I murmur.

Mama continues, seems actually relieved to have the secret out in the open. "I've never said out loud to anyone that I remember another mother before Ganzie."

"Tell me what you remember," I say, strangely no longer angry with her.

"I'm not sure I can talk about it." She looks at me imploringly, her eyes begging, 'please don't do this to me.'

But I can't be discouraged by mere looks. I sit down across the table from my mother and stare directly into her eyes. "Please, Mama," I persist, "I need to know. If you remember," I plead, "say it out loud. Please say it to me..."

She raises her hand to stop my words. Then she speaks quietly as though alone in the room. "It's more of an image than a memory. Sometimes even now I see the face of the woman I think was my real mother, but I wasn't with her very long. I remember she was very pretty and she smelled like glycerin and rose water. But then she left. It was all very sudden. I think she died, but I'm not sure."

"You mean no one ever told you what happened to her?"

"It was not discussed."

"And you never talked about Ophelia to Ganzie or even to your Papa?"

"It was like she never existed, though of course she did. I'm sure she did."

"Did you miss her?"

"It was an awfully long time ago, Neely. I don't recall my feelings."

"How old were you?"

"Four, maybe five. I had just started school and Ganzie bought me a pretty dress."

"What about Charleston Sims. Did you know he was your real Papa?"

"Oh, yes, that I knew."

"How? How did you know?"

"How does one know those things? He was always in my life and I always called him Papa. I never knew another Papa."

"What did you call Ganzie?"

"I always called her 'Mama'. I never made a distinction between her and the woman who smelled like glycerin and rose water. They were both my mama."

42 Alma, 1912

The little girl stood in the doorway with Charleston Sims looming at her side. The house to which he brought her was huge compared to the small rooms where she lived with her Mama. The lady who sat in the cushioned chair was waiting for them to arrive and she extended her arms to the child, beckoning her to approach. She was wearing a dark green cotton dress trimmed in white lace and the little girl could see she was tall and slender. Her brown face--browner than either her own or her Papa's—was not unfriendly but sent a strange shiver through her body.

'What's your name?' Zelle asked, trying to be as gentle as possible.

'Alma,' the youngster answered shyly.

'That's a pretty name. How old are you?'

Alma hesitated for a minute and then held up five fingers.

"Then you go to school.'

'Yes, Ma'am.'

'Good. We'll have to buy you a new dress. Do you like pretty clothes?'

'Yes, Ma'am.'

'Let me show you where you'll sleep,' Zelle said as she led the little girl to the sleeping porch. When Charles made a move to follow, Zelle shook her head in disapproval.

Alone in the living room, Charles paced in despair and frustration. Asking Zelle to take Alma in was the hardest thing he had ever done. Having hurt her once, he was now hurting her again, this time with full knowledge of what he was doing and having no desire to do otherwise. What else could he do? He loved them both and could part with neither.

Feeling the sense of responsibility to a motherless child he hoped she'd feel, Zelle said yes. When she faltered, her Mama and Papa had helped her see it through.

Her Papa said in his most reverent voice, 'God has forgiven Charles for his mistake. Now it's up to us ordinary folks to follow His example.'

Her Mama had held her in her arms and said, 'Zelle, you must do what's right, not what most so-called Christian folks *think* is right.'

Now Alma was actually in their care and all he could do was hope that Zelle would find his daughter irresistible, just as he did.

That night they had supper as a family and, at bedtime, both Charles and Zelle tucked Alma in and each kissed her on the cheek although only Charles took her in his arms, hugged her warmly and held her close.

'We'll take good care of you,' Zelle heard him whisper into the child's ear.

The words sliced into Zelle's heart and she was ashamed of the anger she felt toward the little girl her husband had brought into their home.

Later, in their bedroom, she reproached him.

'I cannot be a mother to that child, Mr. Sims,' she said in a voice, soft, but measured with restraint.

Charles knew when she called him Mr. Sims in that tone of voice, she was very upset even though she seemed calm. But he was upset, too, and was willing to fight for his daughter.

'You can't take your anger toward me out on her, Zelle. If we're going to do this, we have to make her feel at home.'

'That's just the point.' Her voice was louder than before. 'I don't think I can do this.'

'What would you have me to do? I can't ignore my responsibility to her.'

'You shouldn't have lied to me. All those months I didn't know you were visiting her, making her know you as her Papa. How could you do that? And Ophelia! What were you two doing all those times?'

'We've been all through this. I don't have the energy to explain my actions again. I've made many mistakes, but don't make Alma pay for them. She needs us.'

Zelle wanted to scream, 'but what do I need,' but the logic of his words hit her hard, just as he intended. She was, after all, a real Christian woman, not the so-called Christians her mother talked about--and she knew the difference between right and wrong. It was her duty to do what was right, no matter how difficult it might be. She must make the best of the situation as she was expected to do.

When she took Alma shopping, she held her head up high and refuted by her very demeanor, the stares and whispers she knew followed them everywhere they went.

When she took Alma by the hand and led her into the classroom in the very school where she also taught, she again held her head up high and acted like nothing was unusual.

When Charles worked long hours, leaving the mother and child alone together, she acted as a responsible parent, fixing meals, reading bedtime stories, answering questions and bandaging wounded knees.

A sharp tongue, normally so unlike Zelle, a rigid style of discipline and a slight aloofness were the only evidence of the toll the burden she endured took on her spirit.

From the beginning, Alma's natural exuberance got her in trouble with her new mother. Whispering and giggling, laughing too loud, crying too hard, running and playing, dirtying her pretty dresses were all antics that Zelle had no patience for and severely reprimanded.

When Charles tried to intervene, an angry Zelle would silently dare him to say a word. One look from her flashing eyes and he would step away. But at night, when he tucked Alma in, he would hold her close and try to make her forget all the hurt from the previous day.

'I love you,' he would say.

'I've always loved you,' he would say again and hope it was enough.

As time went by, things seemed to come together and he stopped noticing the flaws in their family life. There was no mention of Ophelia or the life that Alma lived before she came to live with her father. All that seemed forgotten...or at least forgiven.

But Charles had a way of not seeing what he didn’t want to see. When things were going smoothly he was content to accept it as reality. Gliding along on a sea of contradictions with blinders on, he didn't have any idea how lonely Alma was nor did he have any understanding of the depth of Zelle’s distress. It might have gone on that way indefinitely but when Alma was about 8 years old, Joe Spencer came to Sedalia and almost took what Charleston Sims assumed belonged to him.

43 A Time to Heal

"Ever since Ganzie told me Ophelia was your mother, I've been in a tailspin," I say.

"I can imagine," Mama replies with the weight of memory pressing down on her words. "It's not something I ever think about or thought I'd talk about. It's like taking my heart and twisting it like a dishrag."

I feel genuinely sorry for the woman for whom I normally have so much animosity. "I didn't tell you to hurt you."

"Why do you suppose she told you?"

"She said she didn't want to die with the secret locked in her heart."

"As usual, she was thinking only of herself."

"No, she wasn't. She was trying to save us."

"Well, she wasn't going to be here to see whether we were saved or not so it was a very selfish thing for her to do."

"On the contrary, it was unselfish and brave. Think how much easier it would have been just to let it stay buried. Secrets destroy. Look what it's done to us."

"Truth destroys, too."

"She knew she didn't show you much love as a child..."

Mama interrupts me vehemently, “Ever! She has never shown me any love. She treated me like a stranger right up to the day she died.”

“Do you have any idea how much Charleston Sims hurt her?”

My mother’s tongue is hot and bitter. “Do you have any idea how many nights I cried myself to sleep because no matter how hard I tried I couldn’t please her?”

“That's just the point. It wasn’t your fault. She wanted you to know that.”

Her acrid tongue is unabated. “A lot of good it does me now.”

“Mama,” I say as gently as possible, “When I think of you and Ganzie, I see you and me.”

“I have never treated you the way Ganzie treated me.”

“Only every day of my life. What have I ever done to make you so angry?”

She seems poised to make a sharp retort, then slowly the expression on her face changes, softens as if defeated. She says quietly, “I do love you, Neely.”

“If you do, I don’t feel it.”

“You were such a headstrong child, always wanting your way.”

“No, Mama, I just wanted to be loved, the same way you did.”

“If you think I was too harsh, you need to know I just wanted you to be strong. I wanted you to be able to make it through this world by yourself, if necessary, not always depending on someone else to take care of you.”

"And you thought criticizing everything I said and did would make me strong?"

"I was only telling you things for your own good."

"Well, you hurt me...badly and I may never be able to forgive you for some of the things you've said to me."

A look of understanding crosses Mama's face. "It is the same, isn't it. Me and Ganzie and you and me."

"Yes, Mama, it's exactly the same and we'll never be able to go back to the beginning to make everything right. But Ganzie hoped we could have a better future."

"I don't mean to hurt you. I want you to know that."

"And I don't mean to be an ungrateful child. We all are more thoughtless than we mean to be."

Mama looks so forlorn and I reach out to touch her arm. "At least you had your Papa. He loved you very much."

"I'm sure he did, I know he did, but sometimes I didn't feel it. He was always so distant."

"He was caught in the middle of two women he loved."

"When Papa died, Ganzie said something so strange but I didn't question it at the time. I was so distraught I just let it go."

She chokes as though she can't bear the memory that has taken hold of her. Her eyes are clouded with sadness and then she closes them as if she can't talk with them open.

"Just before they were going to lower Papa's casket into the ground, she grabbed my arm and said, 'in a few minutes we'll never be able to see your Papa again and all we'll have in this whole world is each other. He loved us both and would want us to take care of each other.'"

"She was trying to reach out to you."

"But I couldn't reach back. We never kissed, we never touched. And then I left."

Then, without thinking about the consequences, I say, flat out, giving the words a life of their own. "What do you remember about Joe Spencer?"

"I never even heard that name."

"He was a man she fell in love with when you were about 8 years old."

"That's preposterous," she asserted.

"Preposterous but true."

"Why would she tell you such a thing?"

"She was trying to help me."

"How in the world did she think that would help you?"

"To let me know that all women are faced with difficult choices—that even in 1915 a woman might love someone different than her husband."

Mama thinks about that for a minute, seems about to say something, then visibly changes her mind.

"What happened to Joe Spencer?" she finally asks.

"Nothing, nothing at all. He left town the next year and that was the end of it. Ganzie stayed with you and Grandpa Charles and made the best of her life."

Anger again creeps into Mama's voice and she says, "Well maybe she should've left with him because she didn't do a very good job of staying."

"But she stayed, that's what counts."

"Staying isn't everything. Look at us."

I look away and say nothing. Maybe staying isn't everything but what is leaving worth?

Then Mama says, "Why do you think she stayed?"

"She always did what was expected of her. She thought that was the right way to live her life. But when she tried to bury her feelings, she made mistakes."

"You know so much about her. I never knew her at all."

"I didn't know her, either, Mama. I loved her but I didn't know her. To me, she was just Ganzie. I only know her secret because she needed to tell someone before she died. And she chose me, hoping it would help us do better than you two did."

Mama looks tired and I'm filled with conflicting emotions, love mixed with outrage and confusion mixed with fatigue. When she speaks, her voice is heavy with regret.

"My life hasn't been easy, you know."

"I suspect not."

"Things don't always go the way we want. They just happen and we adjust."

"I know, Mama," I say compassionately.

"I guess I just adjusted my life away, but it's all I knew."

"I think we should go to bed now, Mama. We can't figure this out in one night."

"I don't know if I can sleep in this house anymore. I feel like a stranger here."

"We are strangers here, both of us. We have to find our way together."

"When did you get to be so grown-up?"

"I've been growing up all along. I just didn't know it until today."

"I've made so many mistakes," she says sadly.

"So have I, so have I. But you know what?"

"What?"

"If we only loved people who didn't make mistakes, we wouldn't love anyone at all."

44 Remembering Sadness

The day after the funeral is strange for us. The mercury soars to 100 degrees and the overwhelming mixture of heat and humidity makes the air unbearable. The lily of the valley and iris planted around Ganzie's porch, normally thriving in the nourishment of good daylight, begin giving up under the duress of the inhospitable climate, their petals shriveling in the torrid sun.

Ganzie's house isn't air-conditioned and the task we have to accomplish under such disagreeable conditions is formidable—to sort through her things and get the house ready to be sold. There is so much to do and perspiration clings to our every movement, making even thinking difficult and tedious.

Throughout the day we work, moving through the small rooms, not talking much, stopping only for a light snack or a cool beverage. I set aside the mementos I want to take back to Des Moines and Mama stuffs plastic bags full of items for Good Will. My progress is exceedingly slow as I find again and again articles that remind me of the past. Tucked away on closet shelves and in dresser drawers are photo albums, scrapbooks and sample after sample of Ganzie's needlecraft.

I also find old record albums still containing 78 rpm records, unbroken and unscratched.

In the kitchen I discover flowered china, sparkling crystal, well-worn cookware, aluminum mixing bowls and more: all of it representing Ganzie's life. Many of the discoveries carry more pain than pleasure as feelings of abandonment and emptiness flood my heart and I get lost in my sorrow.

By evening a light rain has started to cool off the blistery day. I decide it's time to quit and go looking for Mama. I find her sitting on Ganzie's bed, clutching a porcelain vase like it's a lifeline. I stand there for a moment, poised to leave, not wanting to invade her privacy, but somehow have the instinct to stay. I sit down beside her and watch her caress Ganzie's treasure.

"I remember the last time I saw this," Mama says. "It was sitting on the dining room table filled with the first lilacs of spring and I almost knocked it over when I was running through the house. Ganzie scolded me harshly for my carelessness and then put it away for safekeeping. I never saw it again."

"I'm so sorry," I say with genuine compassion but Mama doesn't seem to hear. She is caught up in emotions that are taking her downstream and it is apparent she has more to say.

"I left home as soon as I was old enough to get away," she continues. "The world was less scary than staying here. But what I found out there was not at all what I was looking for.

"I was only 18 when I took a job as a nanny in Kansas City. Papa was upset because I didn't discuss it with him first but I was determined to go and, in the end, he didn't try to stop me."

45 Alma, 1925

It was 1925 when Alma Sims got it in her head to leave Sedalia come hell or high water. She was a spirited young woman, given to bursts of temper, constantly at odds with her mother and growing more and more distant from her father. It was not a time that generated good memories, but it was a time of stubborn determination to show her Mama and Papa that she could make her own way in the world.

At 43, Charleston Sims was already wearied by a life spent living outside of his dreams. Instead of heading his own business, he had settled for working for wages at the railroad yard and taking on odd jobs to make ends meet. He tried hard to hold on to the image of Zelle Marshall he carried in his heart, the beautiful, enchanting young girl he still loved deeply but who no longer resembled the woman at his side. Anger and bitterness had given her soft lips a severe twist and her charming smile was trapped inside that twist. Seldom did they talk of anything other the details of their ordinary days.

Zelle, too, was living a life outside of her dreams but she was more content with her choices. What she had, though not what she longed for when she first saw Charleston Sims that day in June almost 20 years before, was nevertheless strong and dependable. It had survived having its corners tugged and pulled in all directions, sometimes stretched almost to the breaking point. It had survived the temptation of Joe Spencer. Because, after all, that's all he was—a temptation. Nothing more. She had done the right thing by staying, of that she was sure, but some days her relationship with her stepdaughter made her question everything.

So when Alma approached her parents with plans to go to Kansas City, neither wanted her to go, but neither was prepared to talk her out of it.

'I've got a nanny job in Kansas City,' she announced one Sunday after church.

'How in the world did you do that?' Charles asked.

'I answered an ad in the newspaper.'

'How can you get a job all the way in Kansas City just from answerin' a newspaper ad? Don't they have to meet you, talk to you?'

'Well, they did. At least she did. Mrs. Ziegler came to see me last week. I met her at the hotel and we talked. She liked me and said I could have the job.'

'Just like that? She didn't want to talk to your parents or nothin'?'

'I'm 18, Papa. I don't have to ask you if I can go.'

'No, but any respectable family would want to meet your parents.'

'You're old-fashioned. I'm old enough to get a job without my parents say so. The Zieglers are rich and I got a chance to go places and see the world. If I stay in Sedalia, I'll never do anything or be anything. Please, Papa,' she pleaded, 'don't make this hard for me. I need to do something on my own and I don't want to lose this chance.'

Zelle, who had been silent, spoke up finally. She was full of mixed emotions. Even she had been anxious to leave home at age 18 and her sister, Ivy, had taken off for St. Louis as soon as she could get away. No, the wanting to leave, she understood. It was the leaving without a change of heart and leaving without fixing what was wrong that bothered her.

Her brother, Jeremiah, had left that way, taking off for Kansas City without so much as a goodbye. It had broken her parents in two, especially her father who blamed himself for everything that went wrong. Even Joe Spencer had left a trail of unresolved conflict in his wake. Now Alma wanted to leave and she was as defiant as if she had been told 'no' even before she asked.

Of even more concern to Zelle was the fact that the climate in the country had deteriorated and it was not a good time for a young colored girl to be on her own. The hope of racial equality generated by World War I had been stomped and crushed. In the last seven years, lynchings were on the rise and even women were not safe from that wretched crime. Race riots skipped from city to city and nothing was certain.

Furthermore, it was a time of Prohibition and crime was rampant in the cities. Zelle feared for the security of a young, single woman in a huge place like Kansas City. Jeremiah had gone there and had been killed there. No matter how she felt about Alma, Zelle could not easily allow her to leave. Nor could she make her stay. She spoke words she hoped would give her strength and fortitude.

'Of course, you can take the job if you want, Alma,' Zelle said. 'Just remember who you are and how you were raised. Don't ever do anything you would be ashamed to tell us about.'

Charles shot a quick look at Zelle. That was not at all what he wanted her to say. He didn't want Alma to go. He hoped she'd go to college and make something of herself, but he could already tell he wasn't going to have much to say about it. In a rare moment of pique toward Zelle, he wondered if this was her revenge for having to take in a child she didn't want: letting her go without a fight.

'When do you have to go?' he was finally able to ask.

'Mrs. Ziegler said I could come as soon as I could get there. They're planning a trip to Europe in two months and they want me to go with them. They'd like me to get acquainted with the children before we leave.'

There was nothing more to say. Alma was leaving and Charles and Zelle couldn't stop her. They watched her packing her few belongings, both fully aware that somehow they'd have to find a way to live their lives alone together as best they could. Perhaps without the one thing that always pulled them apart, they just might get it right.

It was a sad Charles and a calm Zelle who said goodbye to Alma at the train station. As the engine puffed volumes of smoke into the atmosphere, the three stood on the platform waiting for the time to board. Having his daughter ride the Jim Crow car was humiliating for Charles and he tried to give her, the person for whom he had been willing to sacrifice everything, a few last words of encouragement.

'Write to us, Alma.'

'I will, Papa.'

'And come home if you don't like it.'

'Yes, Papa,' she said. He took his daughter into his arms and held her close.

Zelle kissed her on both cheeks and said only, 'I know you'll do a good job for these people. Just remember what I said. Don't ever do anything you'd be ashamed to tell us about.'

The conductor signaled and it was time to go. The engine whistle blew, smoke chugged into the air and Alma stepped onto the train, taking her life in a direction that she could neither foresee nor control.

"How long did you do work for the Zieglers?" I ask, for the first time in my life interested in something my mother is saying.

"Almost five years."

"And you liked it?"

"I loved it."

"But you were a servant," I say with dismay.

"No, not a servant. I was like part of the family. Of course, I knew my place, but I had lots of freedom and more money than I had ever dreamed about. When the stock market crashed, Mr. Ziegler held on for awhile but eventually had to let me go. Fortunately, I had saved a tidy sum." Alma sighed, "and I used it to start a new life in Des Moines."

"Why didn't you go back to Sedalia?"

"Go back? It never crossed my mind. I still had to prove to Papa and Mama I could make it on my own. Then I met your father...and then you were born. Sometimes you find a place randomly but once you settle down and make connections, you just stay there. You can't keep running forever."

Mama gets up and walks toward Ganzie's room and I follow. She veers off to the living room with me right behind. Looking at her with great intensity, I demand, "How could you marry such a man?" Even without a definition for *such*, she knows what I mean.

She replies as casually as possible, "He was a different man when I met him."

"I hate him."

"If you knew more about what he's been through, you might feel sorry for him instead."

"Why didn't you just leave?"

"You young people today think leaving is the answer for everything. Things aren't working out, you leave. Well, times were different then and it wasn't that simple. I had you and I had a respectable job; I couldn't just risk everything because he wasn't the man I needed him to be."

"But, Mama, you deserved more."

"I was getting what I deserved and I was determined to make the best of it." I look at her with eyes asking for explanation, but she moves away from that thought and instead offers, "Your father and I have never had a good relationship. I knew the first year we were married that I had made a terrible mistake, but I tried to make the best of a bad situation. Some years have been better than others but none have been easy."

"Your terrible mistake affected more than just you."

"You should forgive your father. He's a man with a beast on his shoulders. The women in his life ruined him. First it was his mother, then his sister and then, unfortunately, me. His anger has turned him inside out."

"Did you ever love him?"

"You shouldn't put so much stock in love, Neely. It's not the only reason two people get together. It's not necessary for a good marriage. Sometimes, it's even detrimental."

"Well, love is important to me and I don't want to live without it."

She looks at me with a tight-lipped grimace and says, "Love will only break your heart. All I ever wanted was for you to go through life without a broken heart."

Then she adds, "Maybe Ganzie was right to tell you the truth. Maybe we can't be mother and daughter until you know the whole truth."

The conversation is going in a direction I didn't expect and a chill races through my body.

"You're scaring me, Mama."

"Digging into the past is frightening. That's why most folks carry that stuff to the grave."

46 Alma's Story

Never before have I spoken to anyone about my life and I certainly didn't expect to be confiding in my daughter. The past is long dead and buried and my whole life has been structured to keep it that way. There has never been any reason to resurrect the pain but now that Truth is circling in the air, how can I ignore it?

I loved Neely from the moment she was born, made a great sacrifice to keep her safe, but lived in fear that if God knew how much she meant to me, He would take her back as punishment for my sin. So I tried to make God think she didn't matter all that much. He could take the child but He wouldn't be getting such a prize. And He could never hurt the mother because I didn't care.

It was a precarious tightrope I walked: wanting to hold Neely close yet pushing her away with every angry look; wanting to protect her from harm, yet inflicting pain with every harsh word; loving her so desperately, yet terrified to let it show. If I had known I would lose her anyway, maybe I would have been more courageous.

But how could it have been different? Whatever relationship Neely and I have is the direct result of what I was forced to do to save my own life.

The passing years and the dismal life I live is a testament to the harm secrets can do. The truth no longer holds me in its vise and I want to get it out. Ganzie had the courage to lance a festering wound, hoping it would heal and close forever. Surely, I should try to do the same.

"I'm going to tell you a story that you will not like," I say to Neely. "And when it's over, I hope you'll forgive me."

I've never been more serious in my life as I am when I begin to tell Neely the truth. Nor more afraid. Up to this point, I've done a pretty good job of living my life as though it were never out of control. It may not be a perfect life but it is at least one I've been able to manage. But I don't want Neely to hate me anymore. Maybe if she knows what happened, she'll understand that I did what I had to do under incredibly difficult circumstances.

Would I do it the same way again? I'd like to think not but when you have a life growing inside you and you don't know how you're going to take care of that life, you make choices that you may later regret.

"I left Kansas City because I had no choice. It was the height of the Great Depression and Mr. Ziegler had to close his emporium. I took my savings from its hiding place and headed for Des Moines with Rachel Davis, the Ziegler's cook and my best friend. Times were tough but we heard we could find jobs there and we weren't picky about what kind.

"It was tougher than we thought but we soon found work doing day work for some white folks who still had money to pay for help."

47 Alma and Rachel, 1930

With their meager savings in hand, Alma and Rachel took the bus to Des Moines and found a place to live in a small frame boarding house on 10th Street. They shared a room with each other and the bathroom with three other boarders. It was a far cry from the Ziegler mansion but the rent included one meal a day so at least they knew they wouldn't starve while they looked for work. Times weren't any easier in Des Moines than in Kansas City but within a few weeks both found jobs cleaning houses for the few wealthy white women who still had enough money to pay for day work.

Their days always began and ended with a check for bathroom occupancy and in between, a long bus ride to the city's west side. There, Alma walked north to the Chandler house and Rachel walked west to the Sherman's where they each cleaned all morning and did laundry all afternoon. By 4 o'clock they were off duty and waiting for the bus that took them downtown where they transferred to the line that went down 10th Street. In bad weather, it was depressing, always it was exhausting.

'I got $5.00 extra from Mizz Sherman today,' Rachel chirped one day, tossing the five-dollar bill onto the bed with the odd assortment of coins and bills that represented everything she had in the world.

'Why so much,' Alma asked with envy, assessing her own meager collection of bills and coins.

'She said she liked the way I folded the linens. Can you imagine? White ladies never even say thank you for scrubbing floors and then they pay extra for folding linens. Don't everybody fold linens the same way?'

'Maybe she just likes you.'

'If that's the case, she should just pay me more wages.'

They laughed at the absurdity of even thinking about being paid higher wages for their hard labors let alone the actual possibility. Feeling very much on the bottom rung of the ladder of life, they tried to be content with what they had and feel blessed. Life was much more difficult than it was in Kansas City, but together they survived, together they prevailed.

At supper, the five boarders gathered in the dining room, and for the first time each day, made small talk. Mrs. Cooper hovered over her brood of tenants like the grand matriarch she wanted to be. She was an odd sort of woman, given to frilly dresses and too much makeup, and she served supper with a generous portion of chattering and prying into the personal lives of each person at the table, urging them to talk about their families, their daily activities and their plans for the future.

Gradually over the months little bits of information were put on the table for the others to digest. Alma learned that Millicent Adams was going to college and hoped to be a teacher. She paid for her classes with the wages she earned running the elevator in a downtown department store. Mattie Johnson grew up in Buxton and worked at the hospital, hoping to be a nurse but knowing she was lucky to be an aide. And, after a few months of gracious reticence, Jarvis Priest revealed that he was a writer. By day, he wrote articles for a local colored newspaper and by night, he was tapping out the great American novel on his typewriter.

Alma warmed to the dinnertime chitchat. It was a direct contrast to the somber meals with Mama and Papa, who seldom talked between the saying of the grace and the clearing of the table.

On a night when the winter weather had been especially harsh, Rachel lamented, 'I don't know how much longer I can ride the bus out to West Grand and trudge up that hill and clean the Sherman's toilet day after day. We got to find something different or we'll be doing this the rest of our lives and when we're old, we won't have nothing to show for it.'

That made Alma sad. She thought about what 'different' she could do and came up short. Papa had wanted her to go to college but she would have none of it and now she wasn't prepared for anything other than taking care of other people's children or cleaning their houses.

'I got no skills other than being a nanny and nobody is paying wages for nannies these days,' she said somberly.

But Rachel was not easily discouraged. "There's lots you can do,' she said. 'You're smart and you can learn anything.'

'What about you?' Alma asked. 'What would you like to do?'

'Mattie tells me they's looking for help in the hospital cafeteria. It pays a whole lot better and it's closer to home. I'm thinking about trying for it.'

Then she noticed Alma's downcast eyes.

'Cheer up. We'll get something figured out for you. Remember all the sewing you did for the Zieglers? Maybe you can turn that into something—like taking in mending and alterations. I bet they's lots of folks who'd pay for that. Or you can go to school or you could apply at the hospital, too.

'And then,' she said happily, 'we can get an apartment where we don't have to share a bed...or the bathroom.'

'You're way off in dreamland now,' Alma laughed.

'No, no, I don't mean anything fancy, just bigger with more privacy. What good's our money if it don't make us happy?'

'I'm no good at planning. I just get lost in living day to day. I'm so lucky to have you for a friend.'

'Yes, I'm lucky to have you, too, and coming here is the best thing we ever did.'

48 Starting Over

Rachel got the job she wanted in the hospital cafeteria and eventually convinced Alma to buy a used sewing machine. Zelle had taught her to sew by hand and she had a stitch that was delicate yet strong but the sewing machine allowed her to do mending and alterations without hurting her fingers. Her first client was Mrs. Chandler who was very supportive of Alma's new venture and spread the word to her friends. Soon Alma had more work than she could handle and, to Mrs. Chandler's chagrin, had to cut back on her cleaning duties. When her clients learned she could draft patterns, requests for her services came in fast and furious and she was able to quit day work completely.

Sewing gave her time to brood about what Papa and Mama would think about what she was doing with her life. They had wanted her to become a teacher like her Mama but here she was, sewing for a living. Would they think she was doing the right thing? Or would they think of her as a miserable failure?

Alma could still see her Mama, feet planted firmly on the floor, hands on both hips and fire coming from her mouth.

'You're such a willful child,' she had said.

Alma learned at an early age not to talk back. That was sassing and a resounding slap would surely follow an impudent word.

'Yes, Ma'am,' was all she ever said.

Now past 30, she realized that her willfulness hadn't gotten her very far. It had carried her away from Sedalia on the momentum of an intractable notion but it had landed her on an island of uncertainty with a limited life in front of her.

Opportunities were few for young single colored women with no special skills and good chunks of her savings were gone. With no husband and no education, she wondered what would happen to her when she was old and feeble. Fearing a dismal future, she signed up for courses in shorthand and bookkeeping and made plans to get to find work where her wages didn't depend on her hands.

When World War II threatened, Alma and Rachel had been in Des Moines for almost seven years. The city was flourishing and the minority population had developed a prosperous shadow culture of colored professionals and strong working class men and women. Alma found work in the office of the new black doctor in town and Rachel was all but running the hospital kitchen. With their new prosperity, they moved into a small apartment and when they compared notes, which they did often, they were pleased with their lives and their prospects for the future.

'I wanna be a nurse,' Rachel exclaimed.

'So you can marry a doctor,' Alma said flippantly.

'I'm never getting married,' Rachel protested, 'but you, you could marry Dr. Miller.'

'He's already married, but even if he wasn't, I wouldn't marry him.'

'Why not?'

'Men are such boors. Have you ever seen one of them worth the trouble of putting on your finest dress and combing your hair?'

'Well, not lately, anyway,' Rachel said with a spark of mischief in her eye.

'Not ever, by my count.'

'What are you gonna do if you don't want to get married?' Rachel asked.

'With this job I can do anything I want. Dr. Miller is even having me do some bookkeeping now that he has more money coming in. I don't need anybody but myself.'

Alma's statement came directly from her heart and she said it because she believed it was true. As a matter of fact, it was true right up to the day that Rachel ran into the apartment, slammed the door, threw her hat and coat on the sofa and shouted with great excitement,

'I met someone!'

'What do you mean, someone?' Alma asked cautiously, circling the room like she could escape the words if she kept moving.

'You know, someone special.'

'What do you call special, Rachel?' Alma asked, afraid of the answer.

'You know, a nice young man...'

Except when they were working, they were always together so Alma couldn't imagine how Rachel met someone without her knowing.

'Where, when, who?' she asked, outwardly matching her friend's enthusiasm but inwardly, tense and apprehensive.

They worked hard and had bettered everything about their lives. They didn't have any luxuries but they were certainly on an upward trend. Alma didn't want anything to change. A man in Rachel's life was going to ruin everything.

'At the hospital. Today. He was delivering some supplies and he smiled at me like he kinda liked me. We talked a few minutes and he asked if I was free to go out sometime.'

'You shouldn't talk to strangers,' Alma said haughtily.

'Don't you worry none. He's very polite and absolutely the most gorgeous creature one could imagine.'

'Lucky you.'

'Maybe he's got a friend,' Rachel tried to cajole her roommate.

'I am not interested in a man, so don't go trying to fix me up with one.'

'You never had a man, so how would you know?'

'Correction. Never wanted a man. There's a difference.'

'When you meet Collie, you'll change your mind.'

'Collie? Sounds like a dog.'

'Short for Collier. John Collier is his name but his friends call him Collie.'

'So you're friends already?'

'Alma Sims! If I didn't know better, I'd say you were jealous.'

'No, not jealous at all. Just more cautious than you.'

'You don't have nothing to worry about.'

'When do I meet this wonderful specimen?'

'Saturday. He asked me to go to the movies.'

49 Meeting John Collier

The light rain has turned into a veritable summer storm and heavy drops of water pound the roof and pellet against the windows. Thunder and lightning rule the sky and the wind picks up with frightening velocity. At times it feels like the roof will be carried away into the night and leave us sitting alone in the small house built by Charleston Sims, exposed and vulnerable to the elements. I continue my story with my own thunder and lightning ruling my sky.

"When I met John Collier, I had to admit he was a fine looking man. He was tall and slim like Papa with medium brown complexion and skin smooth as polished stone. A broad nose flattened his face and his full lips were shrouded by a heavy moustache. Also, like Papa, he carried himself in a polite, respectful and soft-spoken manner. I didn't want to like him but I did."

Alma judged all men by her father who was a handsome man by any standards. Few measured up but John Collier had something special. He was actually rather average-looking but when he smiled, his dour expression went through a metamorphosis. A light glowed and sparkled from his enigmatic eyes and his face took on a warm, friendly appearance that drew people close and kept them there. His soft voice charmed and filled his words with kindness and generosity.

She found herself feeling very sorry that Rachel had met him first.

'Collie, this is my roommate, Alma Sims' Rachel said when he arrived that first evening to take her to the movies. 'Alma, this is Collie.'

'Good evening, Mizz Sims,' he replied politely, tipping his hat and bowing slightly at the waist.

His formal mannerisms amused Alma and she decided to reply in kind.

'Good evening to you, too, Mr. Collier,' she said, bending in a mock curtsey. 'Rachel tells me good things about you.'

'I appreciate her kind words.' Then letting his gaze linger on Alma just a fraction of a second too long, he asked, 'Would you care to go to the movies with us?'

Alma had no desire to see a movie or to be an interloper on Rachel's first date, 'No thanks," she replied easily. 'But it's nice of you to ask,' she added to be polite.

Rachel seemed not to notice the exchange between her roommate and her new young man as she gathered her things and prepared to leave.

'I won't be late, Alma, but don't wait up for me,' she said as Collie helped her put on her coat and then guided her out the door.

And then they were gone and Alma was alone with her thoughts about the unwelcome change that was coming into her life quite unexpectedly. She had never given any thought to either her or Rachel bringing a man into their perfect arrangement. And now Collie was a reality and Alma wasn't quite sure how she felt about it.

After that, Rachel and Collie became a regular couple while Alma watched from a distance, feeling very much the outsider. Collie always invited her to join them but Alma always said 'no.' It was bad enough that Rachel couldn't stop talking about Collie; it would be quite another to be a witness to their budding romance. She didn't think she could tolerate seeing Collie looking at or touching Rachel in a way that indicated the direction their relationship was going. So while Rachel was walking on the billowy, white clouds of bliss, Alma was trudging along on the ground, trying not to be resentful of her roommate's new-found happiness.

A few months into their relationship, Collie showed up at the apartment on a night when Rachel had to work. Alma was sure Collie knew she was working but he acted like it didn't make a difference.

'Rachel's not home,' Alma started.

'Yes, I know,' he replied, not moving from the door.

'She's not here, Collie,' Alma repeated more forcefully.

Collie leaned his tall frame against the open door, smiled his broad infectious smile and asked, 'Do you mind if I come in anyway?'

Alma moved aside and let him in, not feeling comfortable in his presence but not knowing how to keep him on the other side of the door without being rude.

'You're a very kind lady,' he said as he entered the apartment, looked around and made himself comfortable on the couch. 'So kind and so pretty. Sometimes I wish I'd met you first.'

'Don't talk like that, Collie,' Alma said, her neck flushing with embarrassment.

'Come sit next to me, Alma," he said softly. 'I don't bite.'

Alma closed the door and moved slowly toward the couch. She sat down at the opposite end but Collie moved to sit closer.

'What are you doing?' she asked in alarm.

'Just noticing how pretty you are.'

'I said don't talk like that and I mean it.'

He reached out and touched her face with his long fingers, calloused from years of hard work.

Alma recoiled and moved out of his reach. 'What are you doing? Rachel is my best friend and I'd never do anything to hurt her.'

'Nor would I,' he replied, touching her face again. Then he smiled, his heavy moustache shielding the mischievous turn to his lip, and said, 'But sometimes there are words that must be said. This is one of those times.'

Then he leaned in to kiss her. 'I think you are one of the most beautiful women I have ever met and I admire how you carry yourself. Most single young women are so hard you can't even talk to them.'

'Rachel's not hard,' she said, pulling away from his kiss.

'No, no, she's not. She certainly is not. She is sweet as a tender ear of corn. You two make perfect roommates. Sweet and kind, confident and strong. Any man in his right mind would have a hard time choosing.'

Then he tried to kiss her again.

'Don't, Collie,' she said, raising her arm as a shield. 'I don't think this is a good way for us to be talking.'

'I know but I can't help it. I been thinking about you a lot lately and I been hoping for a moment to talk to you alone.'

'Collie...'

He leaned toward her again and this time his lips connected to hers and unexpectedly, Alma didn't push him away. Collie, however, pulled himself away. He reached out to touch the side of her face and let his fingers stroke her cheek lightly.

'I'm sorry, Alma. I guess you don't feel about me like I feel about you.'

For a moment, her head yielded to the pressure of his caress and leaned into his hand. At that moment, Collie took a chance and kissed her again but Alma pushed him away.

'Go home, Collie. If you go now, I won't tell Rachel.'

Collie smiled sheepishly. 'I'm sorry,' he said, getting up from the couch and walking to the door. 'I'm sorry,' he said again, then turned on his heel and left.

Alma had never spent any time thinking of herself as a woman and was stunned that Collie had kissed her. When she went to bed that night, she touched her breasts and thighs and felt indecent because her body reacted in a way she didn't recognize. She was surprised that Collie saw her as a desirable woman; she was more surprised to realize she was a woman with desires.

Maybe she was wrong when she said she didn't want a man. That's every woman was supposed to want. How else could she ever hope to have anything in life if she had to get it all by herself?

50 Alma's Regret

A week later, Rachel was working the evening shift and again Collie showed up at the apartment. Alma had spent the week unsuccessfully trying not to think about him and the way she felt when he kissed her. Whenever Rachel chattered about how wonderful he was, Alma shut out her scalding words by repeating the Lord's Prayer to herself over and over.

Now he was in front of her and she realized how much she wanted him to like her. But she also realized her friendship with Rachel meant more to her than anything she might have with Collie.

So she stood her ground.

'You can't come in, Collie,' she said, holding the door to block his tall frame.

He pushed against the door, thwarting her attempt to keep him out. 'I've been thinking about you,' he slurred, the strong scent of whiskey saturating his words.

Once inside, he reached to touch her face but Alma pulled away from his hand. 'You should go," she commanded.

Collie threw his hands up in feigned innocence. "What's a little affection between friends?'

'Please go,' she begged.

He inched further into the breach he had created with the force of his presence. 'I'll bet many a man has been in love with you,' he said seductively.

'That's none of your business.'

'Alma, let me warn you, I'm going to kiss you again. You can slap me, you can throw me out, you can hate me forever, but I'm going to kiss you. And then I'll go away and leave you alone, if that's what you want.'

He took her into his arms and kissed her on the mouth, drawing her lips into his and touching them with his tongue.

'I think I love you,' he whispered.

Alma pushed him away. 'I'm sure you tell Rachel the same thing.'

Collie replied calmly with the assurance that she would not only believe him but understand the depth of his complexities.

'A man can feel love for more than one woman. But a man can only really love one woman,'

'This doesn't feel like love.'

'I would never hurt you, Alma.'

'So you would hurt Rachel instead?'

'We don't have this kind of relationship. She's a sweet girl but I've never told her I love her.'

Alma couldn't separate Collie from his words. He'd held her in his arms, kissed her and said he loved her. His words seemed sincere. Did that make him sincere as well? Did he mean any of it? Could she trust him?

She had accepted isolation as her lot in life and now, she was letting herself be swept away by Collie's touch, his kisses and his dulcet tones.

And she was doing all this with Rachel's man and, what was worse, she didn't care.

But when Collie moved her toward the couch, trying to slide his hands beneath her dress, Alma pulled away. 'No, Collie, we can't do that,' she said firmly.

'I want you to feel what I am feeling. I want to make you happy,' he pressured.

Meeting resistance, he tried harder, weaving his kissing and verbal persuasion into one giant swirl of emotion. Then, holding her tightly, still kissing, still talking, he maneuvered them into a reclining position.

'No, no,' she protested again when his hand began to explore under her dress.

'I won't hurt you,' he whispered into her ear.

'Please, Collie, don't.' She struggled more.

'Let me love you, let me love you, let me love you,' he repeated over and over again and before she could stop him, he was struggling to position himself between her thighs.

Collie on the couch, joined with her in a most unfamiliar, private way, with the fullness of their clothing concealing what was actually happening, was etched on Alma's mind. She would remember forever in alternate waves of shame and pleasure, the way she felt when Collie was moving inside her. She knew nothing about what a woman was supposed to feel when a man was touching her in such an intimate way but what she did feel was a connection for the very first time in her life to another human being.

But when their clothes were restored to order and Collie was sitting back and smiling, Alma felt suddenly alone and deeply humiliated. Allowing John Collier to violate her body did not relieve the emptiness she carried with her every day. Worse, it created a cavity of shame she would never be able to fill.

51 Another Secret

Over the next few months, Collie continued his pursuit of Alma. Showing up at the apartment when she was home alone, he managed to convince her he loved her and just needed more time to break it off with Rachel. Sometimes she said no, knowing full well he was making a fool of her. But sometimes she said yes and these were the times that changed her life forever.

'I'm going to have a baby' she told him on a cold day in December 1939 as they walked through Good Park. She said it simply as if he'd understand and know what he was expected to do. Alma was shivering more from her fear than the frigid weather.

But Collie was totally unsympathetic to her plight.

'You have to get rid of it!' he shouted.

'I thought you loved me!' she shouted back, instantly realizing her mistake.

'Grow up, you stupid...' he snapped but didn't finish his thought.

'You bastard,' she spat at him, her voice full of fury.

'I thought you knew what you were doing,' he rationalized.

'How can you say that?'

Suddenly Collie softened. 'Look,' he said, 'the time just isn't right for us. You have to get rid of it.'

Without saying another word, Alma turned on her heel and stormed away, leaving him standing alone in the freezing temperature. She walked home not having the slightest idea what she was going to do now that she knew Collie didn't love her, would never protect her and that she had to see this one through on her own.

A few weeks later, Rachel announced she and Collie were getting married and Alma finally understood it all. Collie never intended to marry her, had picked her because she was an easy mark. And for being such a foolish woman, it was her punishment to live in shame with the knowledge she gave herself to a man who used her and then threw her away like yesterday's newspaper.

And worse, she was having his child.

All her life, she had wanted to make her Papa proud. Now she had ruined everything with her willful, indecent behavior. Life had lifted her by the nape of her neck and dropped her into a pot of boiling water. Simmering in her own stupidity, she wanted to destroy everything in her path.

'You don't know him,' Alma said, her insides hot on fire and burning out of control.

'I know everything I need to know. Collie is good looking, hard working and a God-fearing man. And he makes me feel special. What more is there to know?'

'Men are scoundrels, Rachel,' she said with acid dripping from her tongue. 'You shouldn't be so trusting.'

'What do you know about it? You've never had a man in your life. You're just jealous when you should be happy.'

'What in the world does happiness have to do with anything?'

Rachel, now frightened, asked, 'What's wrong, Alma?'

'I'm going to have a baby,' she said bluntly, fully aware she was about to destroy their friendship.

'Who on earth is the father?' Rachel asked apprehensively.

'If I tell you, you must believe I never intended to hurt you.'

It was Rachel who now understood everything and a strange sensation crawled up her arms, tingling first, then inflicting unbearable pain. When the words exploded from her lips, they sizzled in the air.

'You slut,' she screamed. 'How could you?'

'I thought he was going to marry *me*.'

'Marry you? You must be out of your mind. Collie is a very old-fashioned guy. He would never marry a woman who puts out. How could you be so stupid?'

'Rachel, please...'

But Rachel was beyond the point of no return. 'Was having a man so important to you that you could forget about me?' she screamed.

'You must believe I never intended to hurt you,' Alma said again, genuinely sorry she had treated her friendship with Rachel with so little care.

'So what did you think I was going to do when I found out? Congratulate you?'

'He said you didn't love him.'

'And that was supposed to make it okay?' Rachel was drowning now in her own desperation. In one fell swoop, she had lost the love of her life and her best friend.

'He lied to us, Rachel,' Alma sobbed.

'He may have lied to us but he corrupted you. You let him make a whore out of you. How could you let him do that?'

'He wants me to get rid of it.'

'I don't want to hear this,' Rachel screamed.

'I don't know what to do...,' Alma tried to speak.

'I said I don't want to hear this.'

'I'm sorry...'

'No, sorry isn't good enough. We can't share this apartment any more. One of us has to go.'

The next morning Rachel packed her few belongings and left leaving Alma to live with her deceit without any hope of forgiveness. Alma was devastated. Losing her best friend was worse than being pregnant by her best friend's boyfriend. She had never been alone, had always had someone to buffer life; now she was on her own, with nowhere to go and no one to talk to. She heard Rachel quit her job and went back to Alabama to live with her mother. Alma could never do that. Going back to live with Mama and Papa was impossible. The last thing they had said was 'don't ever do anything you'd be ashamed to tell us.' She couldn't face them now.

To make matters worse, Collie headed for Chicago and the last time they talked, he blamed her for breaking Rachel's heart.

'You can't have this child, you just can't do it. Everyone will know it's mine and you'll never be able to show your face in public.'

'You should have thought about that when you were cheating on Rachel.'

'You leave her out of this. She never did anything to hurt you and you should be ashamed for what you did.'

52 Alma's Decision

World War II had begun to infect all of Europe when Alma was besieged with the tortures of her reprehensible weakness. There were never going to be enough words to explain what had happened and who did what to whom. She had never had much and now all her possibilities were lost. The baby was all she was ever going to have.

The baby.

Despite her shame, she would never give it up. On the other hand, she didn't know how she'd ever be able to keep it. With her world collapsing all around her, word came that Charleston Sims had died.

It was a bleak January and Des Moines was shrouded under the inhospitality of a wretched winter. The temperature was bitter cold and the day was further crushed by the burden of a heavy snowstorm. The ringing of the telephone was ominous, warning Alma not to answer it. It was late at night, not a time for casual phone calls. She expected to hear the voice of one of her parents and, if she had to choose, she hoped it would be Papa. But it was Zelle and all she said was,

'Your Papa has passed on, Alma. Please come home if you can.'

Stunned, Alma slowly returned the receiver to its cradle carefully as if it would break. A dreadful chill stiffened her spine and her arms encircled her body as if they could hold in some warmth. Sedalia wasn't home. But the cold wasteland of Iowa wasn't home either. She focused on her mother's strange and distant voice, saying, 'Your Papa has passed on.'

Oh God, she cried, what else can You do to me?

The storm had lifted by the time she went to Sedalia to say goodbye to her Papa for the last time ever. The road was narrow and the bus was old. It lurched across the snow and ice islands on the pavement threatening to rip in two any minute. In moments alternating with despair and regret, she wondered if she could tell her Mama about the baby.

By the time she arrived at the door of the house she grew up in, she knew she could not.

Zelle greeted her rather coolly, hugged her only briefly and in the confusion of family and friends, said little to her. It was the same Zelle who always remained aloof no matter how hard Alma tried to reach out to her. It was the same Zelle who stood dry-eyed at the train station when she left Sedalia. And now in the wake of Papa's death, there were still no tears.

The church was filled to capacity. Everyone who had ever known or worked with Charleston Simms came out on the cloudy day to pay their last respects. Alma was calm until she had to pass the open casket. At that moment, reality caught her at the knees. The sight of her Papa's drawn and waxen face, eyes closed, lips tight in a deathly grimace pierced her heart. His hands, crossed at his chest, clutched a Bible and his fingers were thick from years of hard work. He had been such a handsome young man but, in the winter of his life, had grown wrinkled and sallow.

Alma remembered her Papa when he was tall and strong and holding her on his lap, making her laugh, making her feel like she belonged to him. Now she was alone with all her regrets of what should have been, never was and now, would never be.

Only at the gravesite did Zelle attempt to reach out to her. After all the final prayers had been said and there was nothing to do but leave Papa alone in his casket waiting to be lowered into the ground, Zelle moved to her side, laced her arm with Alma's and said softly,

'In a few minutes they'll lower your Papa into the ground and we'll never be able to see him again. All we will have in this whole world is each other. He loved us both and would want us to take care of each other.'

The next day Alma left Sedalia without saying anything about the baby. She had done the very thing her mother warned her not to do– 'Don't ever do anything you would be ashamed to tell us about'– and she couldn't find the words. Vowing never to tell anyone her secret, she forged a plan.

53 Neely

The storm outside only punctuates the storm inside my heart. I glare at Mama, rolls of thunder surging through my body and streaks of lightening shooting from my eyes.

"My father is John Collier," I gasp.

Tears pour down her cheeks and she can barely talk. "Yes," she says barely above a whisper.

"Mama, how could you...?"

"Don't, Neely, please," she begs. "I have lived for over 35 years with this and I can't take it anymore. Your father hates me, you hate me, I even hate myself."

"He's not my father," I say sharply.

"Well, for all practical purposes, he is. He did the best he could under incredibly difficult circumstances."

"Neither of you did very well. You'd have been better off getting rid of me."

"Don't say that. Don't ever say that. You think a woman had many choices back then? You treat life so casually, thinking you can go around doing whatever you want. Well, it wasn't always like that. There were rules, Neely, and I had violated them. What was I to do?"

"You could have loved me, Mama. You kept me so you should have loved me."

"I do love you. I just wanted you to be the opposite of me. I wanted you to be strong so you wouldn't fall for the first man who touched you."

"Well, I'm exactly like you; I did fall for the first man who touched me."

"But he married you..."

"You think marriage is the answer for everything. Is that why you got married?"

"You have to understand how terribly afraid I was."

"What did you do?" I asked apprehensively.

"I met Clement and we got married," she says simply as if it was the natural conclusion to her predicament."

But I see the contradiction and am astonished. "He knew about the baby and married you anyway?"

"He didn't know," Alma replied, unable to look me in the eye.

"How the hell did you pull that off?" I was furious now.

"I didn't pull it off. He finally figured it out and he's never forgiven me. He said I made a fool out of him."

"But he didn't leave you..."

"I told him to leave but he said that would make him even a bigger fool...so he stayed but he's made my life miserable every day since."

"So that's why he hates me," I say sadly.

"No, baby, he doesn't hate you. As a matter of fact, he actually was happy after you were born. I thought he had forgiven me, and then Mae Ella came to town."

I don't think I can take any more surprises but I ask anyway. "Who on earth is Mae Ella?"

"His mother, who abandoned him when he was nothing but a baby. She was a mean, bitter old woman and she expected him to take care of her in her old age. He tried to do the right thing by her and she poisoned his mind with her hatred of me. He was never the same after that."

In a few short days, I have heard more truth than anyone should hear in their entire lifetime. Ganzie's truth was one thing. But this is a truth of biblical proportions and it's more than I can take.

"So I come from a long line of emotional cripples," I scream, then lurch from Ganzie's bed and race to the sleeping porch. Grabbing my suitcase, I start throwing my clothes into it. My face is a mixture of anguish, determination, fear and anger.

Mama follows me and when she sees what I'm doing, she demands, "Where are you going?"

"I have nothing else to say to you, Mama."

"I asked you where are you going?"

"I don't know but as far away from you as I can get."

"You are such a hateful child."

"I know and you made me that way."

Frightened, Mama follows me as I dash about the house collecting my things and then start lugging them out to my car. The rain is soaking everything in sight and the tree branches hang low with the weight of moisture. She watches helplessly from the porch as I stuff in one load after another.

"You can't leave me here," she shouts, crying visibly. "How will I get home?"

I stop what I'm doing and look up at her. Through the foggy rain, the light from the house casts a reflection across her face in stripes of illumination. The rain cascades down over my body until my clothing is soaked. I am crying like I'm sad but I'm actually spitfire mad.

"Please, Neely," she begs from the porch.

For a moment I reconsider my decision to leave. Then I don't care anymore.

"Goodbye, Mama," I say as I climb into the car.

I pull out of the driveway and speed up the street, away from Ganzie's house, away from my despicable mother, away from Sedalia and away from the unvarnished truth.

54 The Party's Over

Over the next few days, my emotions escalate out of control and my body breaks apart at all its fault lines. Ganzie's death still hangs over me like a fish net trapping me inside and my indecision about Gill weights me down. And in middle of my struggle to break free, I don't have the ability to absorb the surprises that have been hurled at me out of the blue: that Ganzie is not my real grandmother and Clement Kingston is not my real father.

One I love, the other I hate; yet both are an integral part of my life and neither can be discarded without slicing me into pieces. And there's no one to talk to, no one to help me put myself back together again. The only person who could do that is gone.

Ganzie I understand. She got caught in the expectations of her Papa and didn't know how to make things right. The secret let her keep her dream and I can forgive her for that.

But to excuse my mother's transgression will take more charity than my heart can hold. She has turned my world upside down. How dare she not tell me who my real father is?

Never explain to me why Clement Kingston treats me like an outsider?

Going to see Gill with my lungs filled with poisonous air and my stomach knotted into a closed fist is not the best idea. But it's time to face him and, if nothing else is accomplished, it will distract me from my current anguish.

I pull myself from my rumpled bed, throw on some clothes and dab my face with makeup to try to conceal my swollen eyes. In a daze, I drive to the office and am finally face to face with the man I don't want to love any more.

"You don't have to quit," Gill says, leaning back in his chair and watching me disintegrate before his eyes. I have spilled out the whole saga to Gill's impatient ear ending with my decision to quit the agency.

Now I stand by his expansive window and watch the traffic below waiting for him to say words that will make me feel whole. My own words waver in and out of coherency.

"I can't work right now. I can't even think anymore."

"But you don't have to quit..."

I cut him off before he can finish that thought. "I need to get away from this job and..." I can't finish the sentence. But Gill knows me well enough to figure out where the conversation is headed.

"...and what? Me? Is that what you don't want to say? You need to get away from me?"

"I told you we shouldn't have mixed business with pleasure."

Gill looks wounded but quickly recovers. "It just happened...I won't apologize for it," he says sharply, then tries to lessen the harshness of his words. "Maybe you just need some time."

"I don't know if time will help. It even hurts to breathe."

"You're stronger than you think you are." His voice takes on a tone that pushes me away rather than bringing me closer.

"Nobody is stronger than they think they are," I sob, my body literally sagging from the weight of my distress.

"If you look in Webster, 'all screwed up' is the definition for family. Do you think you're the first person to find out there's some skeletons in the closet?"

"I thought you'd be more understanding," I snap with anger overtaking my sorrow.

He tries to be tough on me. "Understand this--if you cave in now, you'll regret it for the rest of your life."

I have seen Gill be hard on other people; I don't like him trying that with me. "I understand this," I say hotly, "if I hang around you much longer, I'll regret that for the rest of my life."

The exchange is spinning in a downward spiral that neither of us knows how to stop.

"Don't let this thing turn you into a mean, bitter woman," he says flatly.

Hearing the words that Mama used to describe Mae Ella, I explode. "I knew you were too much like Roland to be any good for me."

In a more conciliatory tone, Gill offers, "Six months from now you'll look back on all this with a different eye. Give yourself a chance to reach that vantage point."

"I'll let you know where to send my last check..." I turn sharply and storm out of Gill's office leaving him enveloped in a stunned silence.

I hear a crash and know he's thrown something against his office wall. I know he's hurting and I almost go back to wrap my arms around him and tell him I'll be okay soon but then decide leaving is the best thing I can do for both of us.

55 Clement Kingston

Clement Kingston has never been a person I could run to with my troubles. He is a sour-faced, heavy-set man, with thinning hair and a flabby jowl. His brown skin is splotched with age spots and he looks older than his chronological years. Now retired from a lifetime of unimportant jobs, he can be found most of the time in front of the television, reclining in his favorite chair, puffing on a well-smoked pipe. Seldom interacting with the women in his life, he likes his beer frosty cold and his frequent naps uninterrupted.

Nevertheless, I steer my car in the direction of my parents' home, needing to talk to my father, knowing it's probably a mistake. But he's the only person I can think of who might be able to make my world stop spinning out of control. There are too many missing pieces to the puzzle and only he can provide the clue.

But Clement Kingston is not known for his concern for my anguish. All through my school years, when I wanted anything he considered frivolous, he treated me like the wicked stepchild.

Even when I wanted to go to college, he offered no support.

'Got no money for college, Neely. I work hard for my money and got no extra for frivolous things.'

He was planted staunchly in his recliner while Mama sat motionless on the couch. I was crumpled on the floor, begging with my eyes.

'Daddy, please, this is important,' I say.

'If it's so important, what's wrong with gettin' a job? I'll tell you what--you want everything given to you on a silver platter.'

Mama interceded. 'Clement, this is pure nonsense. You could come up with the money if you wanted to.'

'You've never been able to handle money so what do you know?'

'That's not true and you know it but that's not the point.'

'Look, she's always wantin' something. First it was piano lessons, then art supplies, then a prom dress, then party shoes. It never ends...'

Later, I was alone in my room, lying on my bed, staring at the ceiling, feeling like my world had come to an end. Mama entered the room without knocking, as was her custom.

'Your father says he'll give you money for the first year. If you keep your grades up, he'll consider the rest.'

'What did you say to get him to change his mind?'

'It doesn't matter what I said. The important thing is that now you got what you wanted, don't blow it.'

Now almost two decades later, I approach my father, knowing I have blown everything as far as he is concerned. He is sitting in the same recliner he's been ensconced in for twenty years. I perch on the edge of the couch and watch him intently.

"I don't hate you, Neely," he says in response to my accusation.

"You treat me like you do."

"I know I'm not a very good father and I don't offer any excuses. Sometimes a man is full of things even he don't understand."

"Do you hate Mama?"

"Hate? That's too strong a word. We just tried to make something work that really didn't have a chance. If she'd told me the truth, I prob'ly would've married her anyways--I loved her that much. But when somebody lies to you like that, it makes you feel like a fool. I didn't like that feelin' much."

I look at the only man I know as my father and all I see is a tired, old, dispassionate man whose spirit has been completely decimated by years of cantankerous living.

"You didn't have to take it out on me."

"What do you want me to say? That I'm sorry? Of course, I'm sorry but what good does that do now? I am what I am and you are what you are."

"What about Mama? What is she?"

"That's between me and her and I don't guess there's any truth to save us. We already know all the truths and all the lies."

"I wish you'd been a drinking man...at least I could understand that."

"I wish I'd been a drinkin' man, too. Might have made my days a whole lot easier." He takes a draw off his pipe and says, "Look, Neely, what do you want from me?"

"Everything I thought I knew has been snatched from me. I want to make some sense out of it. I thought maybe you'd stop being selfish for a minute and help me."

"You always wanting everything handed to you on a silver platter and then you cry when you don't get it."

My face fills with rage. "That's not true," I sputter.

"You left your husband, you abandoned your mother in Sedalia and you quit your job...you keep runnin', you keep burnin' bridges...you not gonna have anything to come back to. If I was you, I'd settle down and figure out how to live the rest of my life before I made another bad decision..."

56 Running Away Part II

With nowhere to go and no one to talk to, I check out of the hotel, load the VW with my few belongings and head north on Interstate 35. I'm headed for the last place Gill and I spent together but I'm not sure why I think that will help. I just know I need to be anywhere but here and I drive obsessively and relentlessly, every mile taking me further away from everything that hurts.

The rhythms of the highway create patterns that talk to me, tell me about the absurdity of what I'm doing. The wind noise whistles, "get things figured out." The softly purring engine murmurs "I have faith in you." And the tires pounding against the pavement say, "go home." In the puff of clouds clinging to a corn blue sky, I see Ganzie's face and I know I'm not alone.

I've driven over 50 miles before I realize that I'm trying to run away from home again but this time I don't have any place to go. By leaving, I'm escaping nothing; all will be waiting for me when I return.

Who am I to be so judgmental about another's faults? Who am I to criticize Mama and Daddy when they gave me more than they ever gave themselves? Who am I to be angry with Roland when I'm the one who allowed him to ruin my life? And who am I to be so cruel to Gill when all he wants to do is give me love?

And then I finally get it figured out.

It's nobody's fault.

And nobody should have to take the blame.

Everybody does the best they can at any given point in time. They don't always have what they need at the precise moment they need it. Maybe there's evil in the world but nothing that happened to Ganzie, to Mama or to me happened because of evil. It happened because of the fragility of the human spirit.

I turn around and head for home and I'm much calmer on the return trip.

I stop at a gas station, find a phone booth and place a call. After a few short seconds, I hear Mama's voice on the other end of the line.

"Mama, it's me. It's been a rough few days but I think I understand things a whole lot better now. I've got no place to stay. Can I come home?"

"You can stay in your old room until you decide what to do next," she says.

"What will Daddy say?"

"Don't worry about him. This is my house, too, you know."

57 Redemption

When I arrive at the old frame house on Boyd Street, Mama opens the door and I reluctantly cross the threshold of Clement Kingston's house. He is as usual stretched out in his recliner, watching television and chewing on his pipe. He grunts when he sees me and peers disapprovingly over his reading glasses.

"It'll be all right, Neely," Alma reassures. "I've talked to him and he's okay with it."

I've been gone for over 15 years, but my room is exactly the way it was when I was a teenager. Nothing has been moved or changed. The furniture is still in the same places and the curtains and bedspread have not been replaced. On the bureau, all the trinkets from my high school days still rest on of one of Ganzie's crocheted doilies. On the nightstand beside the twin bed is the baby blue Princess telephone I begged for. Daddy refused to let me have it but the next day Mama went to the phone company and got it for me anyway. Funny, how I never remember the nice things she did for me.

I sit on the bed and pat for her to sit next to me.

"I'm sorry I left you in Sedalia." The words come out awkwardly and I let out a nervous laugh.

"It's all right," she replies, "I deserved it."

"We all deserve better than we sometimes get."

She doesn't reply leaving me alone with my apology.

"I know your life hasn't been easy..." I continue.

"Life is not just an idea or a hope or a dream. It's the real thing and I live each day with the reality of what I've done."

"I don't blame you for anything. I don't blame anybody for anything. We've all made mistakes and we should just move forward, not look back."

"I know my words come out twisted and angry. I don't want to be like that anymore." She pauses, then says "I'm going to leave your father."

I am totally shocked and I don't hide it. But then I feel such a sense of relief. "He won't last a minute without you."

"The only way I can make up for the pain I've caused is to stop causing it."

I look at the stranger who is my mother and wonder if we are becoming friends. I wonder if I can trust the new women we're trying to become.

"Ganzie will be glad we talked," she says.

I smile. "Yes, she will," I reply.

"I loved her in spite of everything. I want you to know that."

"And I love you, Mama," I say, kissing her forehead.

I sleep well. Perhaps it's exhaustion from the trip, perhaps it's being in my familiar room, or maybe because for the first time in forever, I feel peaceful inside knowing I'm strong enough to make my own way through life.

58 The Road Taken

I'm back in bed, half asleep when the doorbell chimes. I got up early to have coffee with Mama before she went to her volunteer work at the nearby elementary school. Not ready to face the day, I retreated to the sanctuary of my room with plans to scour the want-ads and to make lists of things I need to do. Instead I bury my face in the pillow that absorbed so many of my childhood tears and curl up in much the same way I did when I was young and feeling vanquished from the world.

I wait a few seconds, hoping Daddy is still home. One thing I've learned since I've been here is that he doesn't actually sit in his recliner all day. On the contrary, he goes for walks every morning, then putters around the house fixing things, works in the yard and does odd jobs for neighbors whenever he's asked. He spends a lot of time at the hardware store and the auto supply store. I've paid no attention to what my parents do now that they've retired and it appears they both have busy days.

Funny how your mental image of someone is based on how you feel about them. If you love them, your thoughts are gentle; if you don't, your thoughts are wrapped in barbed wire.

The doorbell chimes again but still I don't move because it can't possibly be for me. Then that thoughtless unseen finger presses on the doorbell insistently, chiming first at regular intervals and then in one long, continuous reverberation.

Who is so impatient? The police? A neighbor in trouble? Thinking it must be important, I reluctantly trudge downstairs and open the door. When I see Gill standing on the porch, I snap, my voice salty with anger, "How did you know I was here?"

"Your mother called me. She said we should talk."

I know Mama is only trying to help but she's put me directly in the headlights of an oncoming Mack truck. I decide to meet it head on rather than delaying the impact until later. It's the only way I can end the threat and maintain my new-found equilibrium.

"Gill," I say firmly, extending my arm and raising my hand defensively, "I've given this a lot of thought...and nothing's changed."

He replies sarcastically, "You look good, too, Babe."

"Whatever we have to say to each other, this isn't the right time or place."

"This is exactly the right time and the right place. If we don't talk today, we might never talk again."

"For the first time in my life, I'm going to do what's best for me and I don't think I'm ready to be with you...or anyone."

"You could at least talk to me...give me a chance to change your mind."

"I don't want my mind changed."

"What about your job? Are you going to throw away your career just like that?"

"I quit my job, remember?"

I step onto the porch to keep Gill outside. If he comes in the house, sits down on the couch, looks at me in a certain way, touches me even, my resolve might melt. Even on the porch, I am extremely uncomfortable and my skin prickles with the awareness of his proximity. I clasp my arms tightly around my shaking body to hold it still.

"What do you want to talk about?" I ask with a strategic hostility lacing my words.

He looks serious, almost angry, when he says, "I don't want to end it, that's what. I want us to have a chance to develop this flame between us into something that will burn for the rest of our lives."

"That's very poetic, Gill, but flames don't last that long. Eventually they die out."

"That's because most people don't know how to keep them burning."

I step off the porch into the warm morning air and walk away from Gill at a crisp pace. He has to take long strides to keep up.

"My grandmother..." I say, my words matching the rhythm of my brisk steps, "married a man she adored and he treated her love like dirt, like he could do whatever he wanted and she would stand by him. And you know what, she did."

"Wait," Gill says breathlessly, extending his hand to stop me.

I turn and glare at him. "It was expected of her. Even when she fell in love with a man who adored her, she gave him up because it was expected of her."

I march away from him, continuing to spit words into the air in front of me.

"My mother...she got pregnant by a man who used her and threw her away...and she almost died of the shame...which probably would have been a whole lot better than living with the shame. It pushed her into a marriage to a man who treats her like dirt... I don't want my life defined by a man...period."

Gill catches up to me and grabs me by the shoulder, stopping me at the edge of the driveway.

"That was all a long time ago...."

I interrupt him, "To me, it's like it just happened yesterday. The choices they made make me who I am today."

"That's where you're wrong. The choices you make, make you who you are today."

"I can't run away from my past."

"Nobody can, Neely, but the past is only a guidepost, not a definition. What you gotta do is live in the present, then run like hell toward the future."

"Don't lecture me, Gill. I don't need anybody to tell me what to do."

I pull away from him and continue walking down the sidewalk. He catches up to me again.

"I always gave you credit for being a strong lady. That's one of the things I love about you."

"I'm not strong at all but I'm going to stop being stupid."

"Sure you got weak spots. Don't we all! Sure you've made bad choices. Sure you trusted the wrong people." He holds his right hand up to acknowledge his own culpability. "Guilty! That doesn't mean you aren't strong. It just means you're still a work in progress. But you keep moving in the right direction and you keep fighting for what you want. That's what being strong means."

I stop in the middle of the sidewalk and turn to Gill with my body shivering with all my twisted up emotions.

"Go home, Gill, go home...Please..."

"If that's what you really want, that's what I'll do. I've never stayed anywhere I wasn't wanted."

He turns to leave, walks a few steps, then looks back. I know he wants me stop him but I won't. My life is just too confusing to make things work with him. I'm just resolving issues with Mama and Daddy; I can't fit Gill into the picture.

He walks a few more steps, looks back again but I stand stubbornly in place, refusing to even acknowledge his going, but my body is caving in on itself and he sees it.

Without hesitation, he comes back to me.

"Let's not do this, Neely," he says, gently, patiently, lovingly.

"What would you have me do? I can't do things your way."

"I've never wanted to control you; I've never wanted to own you. I may be an arrogant, selfish son of a bitch with most folks but when I'm with you, I'm different...and I like who I am when I'm with you." He reaches out and touches the side of my face.

"Do you love me, Neely?" he asks.

"I told you, love isn't enough."

More forcefully he asks again, "Do you love me, Neely?"

"Of course, I do..."

"Then don't disappear on me again," he says, leaning into me and kissing my forehead, then each cheek then my lips.

"Don't ever disappear on me again," Gill whispers with his lips touching mine and his arms holding me close.

EPILOGUE

Everything you might have expected to happen, did. I went back to work at the agency, divorced Roland and eventually married Gill. In spite of my deep feelings for him, it was not an easy decision. Ganzie said it best: trust is more important than love and it took me a long time to trust, not him, but myself. Trust that I would not knowingly put my foot in a bear trap, trust that I would even recognize the bear trap in the first place, trust that I didn't actually like bear traps in some perverse sort of way.

Somehow through all the drama, Mama and Daddy found their harmony and she stayed with him. Maybe it was because in her older age, she didn't really have any place else to go. But I like to think it was because they really cared about each other and the lancing of the wound that had festered in their lives relieved the pressure that was pulling them apart. Both are gone now and every day, I pray that they're truly resting in peace.

Gill and I have a daughter and her name is Sarah, named after Ganzie's mother. And she has a daughter who she named Zelle. So the branches of our family tree continue to grow from a foundation rooted deep in family secrets. Both Sarah and Zelle know all the stories of Charleston Sims, Opelia Lucas, Joe Spencer and John Collier because I believed it was important for them to know their history but Sarah wasn't so sure. She said it made her feel unsettled. She considered it all nothing more than gossip and would rather not have known the transgressions of her ancestors.

On the other hand, Zelle, who just turned 15, is blessed with the wisdom of the Millennial Generation—she really doesn't care.

"They're good stories, Grams," she says, "but what difference does it make? It's too bad they had to suffer so for things that, in the end, don't matter all that much." This is totally understandable coming from a young woman who is the child of a single mother, lives every day with the terms, 'baby momma' and 'baby daddy' and thrives in a culture that isn't destroyed by shame.

But they do matter, maybe not in the vast eons of eternity, but in the brief spans of history that we occupy, they matter because we can't see the future and we don't know it will all be forgotten. And, if not forgotten, will lose its grip on us. But while we're caught in the vise, we have to figure it out. That takes time, takes energy and takes its toll.

I hold up the photograph of Charleston Sims and Zelle Marshall so my granddaughter can see it clearly. Over one hundred years have gone by since it was taken and all the ravages of time are evident in its frayed edges and fading image.

Zelle Sarah Howard stares at her great-great-grandmother, Zelle Sims, and exclaims, "Gosh, she was a beautiful woman."

"She was more than beautiful," I say reverently. "She was strong and independent and she meant everything to me."

"I know you must have loved her 'cause you talk about her all the time, almost like she's still here."

"She is, Honey. I feel her with me every day."

"That's creepy, Grandma?"

"No, it's just the power of love."

"I don't understand that kind of love."

Just then Gill enters the room. "How's my ladies?" he asks.

"Zelle here is just questioning the power of love. She doesn't believe that love is eternal."

"Baby, you just haven't felt it yet. But when you do, you'll know it. I love your grandmother that way and that's the way she loves me."

Gill is retired now and his health is poor. Every day, I worry about losing him but also every day, I'm thankful I found him. I try to concentrate on the finding and push the prospect of losing away.

We have now been married for almost 35 years, longer than Ganzie and Grandpa Charles were together. But in this sense, history did not repeat itself: Gill and I found the secret to staying together and being happy. Between the relentless hours and the fleeting minutes of the spaces where we lived, the times that usually slip by unnoticed, we have paid attention. Attention to the moment, attention to the hour, attention to each other.

We have not always agreed on how to manage our lives, sometimes quite bluntly, but I can honestly say, he has never mistreated me. It helps, of course, that I don't see mistreatment in every glance and I don't feel the need to lash out at every frustration.

I guess if I had one last thing to say it would be this: I am at peace with myself. My life has been a series of small catastrophes all linked together by exquisite crystalline moments, dangling like amulets on a charm bracelet and, when I'm alone with my thoughts, it's these moments I remember most.

Probably the most trivial thing I can say right now is that if I could live my life over again with the knowledge I have now, I would do it all differently. There's tremendous catharsis in the words "If I could do it over, I would do it better."

But would I?

And, given how well my life has turned out, would I even want to?

If such things are possible, Ganzie is smiling down on me.

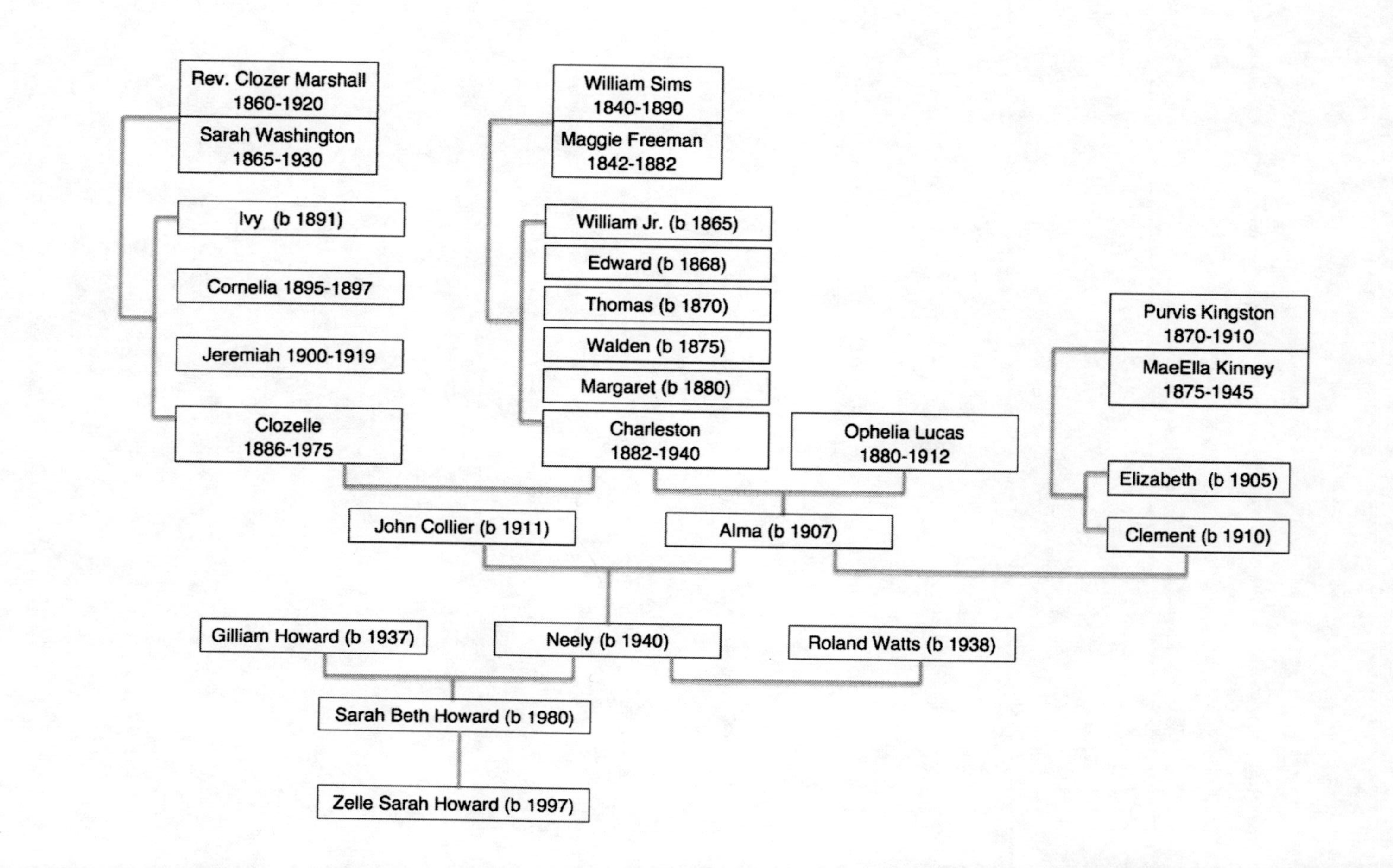
Rev. Clozer Marshall
1860-1920
Sarah Washington
1865-1930
Ivy (b 1891)
Cornelia 1895-1897
Jeremiah 1900-1919
Clozelle
1886-1975
William Sims
1840-1890
Maggie Freeman
1842-1882
William Jr. (b 1865)
Edward (b 1868)
Thomas (b 1870)
Walden (b 1875)
Margaret (b 1880)
Charleston
1882-1940
Ophelia Lucas
1880-1912
Purvis Kingston
1870-1910
MaeElla Kinney
1875-1945
Elizabeth (b 1905)
Clement (b 1910)
John Collier (b 1911)
Alma (b 1907)
Gilliam Howard (b 1937)
Neely (b 1940)
Roland Watts (b 1938)
Sarah Beth Howard (b 1980)
Zelle Sarah Howard (b 1997)

Acknowledgments

BRANCHES has been a labor of love for at least the last 15 years and owes its existence to a nugget of a truth that was revealed to me many years before that. It has endured many re-writes and along the way, a lot of good souls read, re-read, edited, re-edited, encouraged and re-encouraged to keep the story alive. I particularly want to thank my friends at the University of Northern Iowa, Kathy Oakland, Vickie Robinson and John Quinn, who helped me get the manuscript off my closet shelf and encouraged me to get it published. Especially John, who was a Creative Writing instructor and told me that he loved it because it was "not a chick flick" and helped me develop the character of Alma. I also must thank Jeff Schmidt, a literary agent, who once told me the story "really delivered" and encouraged me to edit it to perfection and even suggested I write BRANCHES, the screenplay.

Along the way, my nieces, Jean and Theresa, have read various versions and given me support and encouragement. And if it weren't for Jean, the chapters would not have names, a true enhancement to the story. Others in my extended family have also supported and encouraged my writing ambitions for more years than anyone would care to count.

Honorable mention goes to Stephanie Corbett because out of a conversation with her a nugget of an idea was planted that publishing on Amazon was doable and desirable.

Tangela Scott-Jones deserves my thanks because she took my last rewrite and helped me edit all the changes that took the story from 3rd person past tense to 1st person present tense.

Without her edits and encouragement, I'd still be struggling with consistency and continuity.

Lennox Randon, my nephew and fellow author, deserves my greatest thanks because he took BRANCHES from my computer to the world. His knowledge of formatting, style and CreateSpace has given reality to my dream.

ABOUT THE AUTHOR

Rebecca Sloan is the author of four novels, three screenplays, hundreds of poems and a dozen short stories. BRANCHES is the first of her works to be published.

She lives in Lakewood, Ohio, with her daughter and works as an Account Clerk at Case Western Reserve University.

ABOUT THE ARTIST

Rebecca Star Haviland was born and raised in Cleveland, Ohio. Her art reflects her spirit: "I was taught love and respect for nature and all her beauty. I am inspired by the changing seasons, colors, smells, sounds, memories and dreams. My work represents moments that nature has shared with me when I stop and look at her."

CPSIA information can be obtained at www.ICGtesting.com
Printed in the USA
LVOW08s0305281013

358869LV00001B/77/P